I0563438

Falsely Accused

The Billionaires' Club Series: Book 9

AE Moran

The Invisible Publishing Company

The Billionaires' Club Series

Contents

Chapter 1: Diego

I shake hands with Kevin Drake and pat him on the shoulder. "Look at you! You're glowing! Marriage suits you."

He blushes and bites back a grin. "You have no idea."

I turn to his lovely wife, Paige Novak, and press her hand between both of mine. "And you! Look what you've done to our calm, cool, collected Kevin! I've never seen him blush so much. Only you could do this—and now I can't even kiss your hand anymore. I would gouge out my eye in that enormous rock on your finger."

She laughs at me. "We wouldn't want that."

I wave to the table behind me. "Sit down, sit down. Montgomery and Emerson will be here any minute now."

I sit down on one side of the conference room table and they sit down on the other. We all take out our devices.

"So the SigmaTech contract is going well with the Pentagon," I begin. "I haven't heard any noise from you that they're causing you any further problems."

"No, thank you, Diego," Paige tells me. "Your intervention was invaluable. We're in your debt."

I laugh and wag my finger at her. "You're hardly in my debt—not after the money you made me with this contract. Now the reason I wanted to talk to you both was because I have a new contract proposal you may be interested in."

I turn my laptop around to face them, but Montgomery Sinclair and his son Emerson come in just then. Montgomery is a tall, strong, white-haired silver fox not much different from Dante Helme. Montgomery might be a shade younger. I don't really know.

He also has a much flintier personality. Dante is a pussy cat. Everyone loves doing business with him—and everyone does do business with him.

It takes a certain kind of finesse to do business with Montgomery. He has a fiery wit and doesn't spare the verbal artillery when it's called for.

He also doesn't stand for any hanky-panky in his business dealings. He's very vocal in announcing to the world when he thinks someone isn't smart enough, savvy enough, or honest enough to do business with him.

His attitude has earned him his share of enemies among people who aren't smart enough, savvy enough, or honest enough to do business with him. A person has to be pretty high up the food chain to meet his standards.

I have no problem with that. I have never had a problem doing business with Montgomery. We've been partners for years.

His son Emerson is a quiet, watchful sort with soft brown hair and piercing brown eyes. He isn't as tall and intimidating as his father and Emerson is alert to everything. His quiet, reserved manner hides an edge of danger as hard and unyielding as Montgomery's.

Emerson is more socially adept, though. He can keep his opinions to himself when it suits him. He doesn't go around pissing people off. He doesn't usually tell anyone what he really thinks. He keeps that to himself, too—which is an important skill to have in business.

I like them both. Montgomery is training Emerson to take over the business once Montgomery isn't able to anymore. Emerson watches everything his father does and learns from it—both the good and the bad.

Emerson learns from everyone and everything. He never misses anything. God only knows what damning information he keeps stored upstairs in his head. I would shudder to find out.

Paige and Kevin shake hands with both Montgomery and Emerson. The five of us have been doing business ever since Paige moved to New York with SigmaTech, her state-of-the-art medical equipment company.

I've been doing business with Kevin for years before that, but the two of them only teamed up with this joint offering recently. Paige is good for business. She's good for everyone's business.

Montgomery and Emerson sit down with me on my side of the table and we all face each other while I go through our new offer.

"It's another contract for the Russians." I flip through a bunch of documentation from the Russian military. "They want us to sell them the equipment and for you to train their personnel. We also have the Chinese on the hook. They just haven't explicitly offered a contract the way the Russians have."

"Um...." Paige and Kevin exchange glances. "Wouldn't that be kind of illegal?" Paige asks. "The US military has already accused us once of threatening the United States' interests by withholding information about this equipment for them to study. The Pentagon would have an aneurysm if they found out we were selling to the Russians—let alone to the Chinese."

"As to the second matter, you've already sold the equipment to the US military, so you wouldn't be doing anything different by selling to any other organization on the planet," I tell her. "I would also remind you that multiple international organizations have already acquired this equipment from you and could theoretically be studying it for the purpose of replicating it. The militaries of the world aren't unique in that. That's simply the risk you take by selling your product to anyone."

She shrugs. "Okay. I get your point."

"As to the first point, we would use our channels in Europe to circumvent any laws—which there are no such laws that prohibit you from selling medical equipment to the Russians. I can think of a dozen other American companies who are already doing it. Our corporate structure is based in Europe, so technically, we would be the ones acquiring the equipment from you and selling it along to the Russians—which is how we make our money."

"What about the personnel?" Kevin asks. "We're talking about training a whole lot of Russian military personnel and potentially members of the Chinese Army. I'm going to go out on a limb and suggest that the US government won't take it very kindly if we bring these foreign personnel over here. The government could very well just deny these people visas and our deal would be dead in the water."

Paige turns to him. "What about setting up training centers overseas? You've already talked about doing that. This could be the perfect opportunity. You could do it in neutral countries or ones that are more agreeable to you doing business in their country no matter what the nature of that business is. I'm sure you can find countries closer to both Russia and China that have better relations with them than we do."

Kevin raises his eyebrows. "True. I could do that."

"What matters is that we get this equipment to the people who need it," she goes on. "I really don't care what nationality they are. I agree with you, Diego. Selling medical equipment and training medical personnel isn't a crime nor is it undermining the United States' security interests. I think we should go for it."

"I'll send you the details," I tell her. "And Kevin, you'll need to start putting the wheels into motion to set up your training centers or whatever it is you need to do. You'll need to have all of this in place as soon as the contract goes ahead."

"I'll do that." Kevin glances back and forth between me and Montgomery. "Is that all? Are you sure you don't want us to start supplying the Martians with medical equipment next?"

I laugh. "Not them, but we are getting some very unusual requests from certain.....let's be diplomatic and call them black organizations who shall remain unnamed."

"Then you can tell your counterparties that they'll need to create front groups for themselves to deal with us," Paige interjects. "Tell them to pass themselves off as civilian organizations and we won't have any problem."

I nod. "That is what I am telling them. I think a few of them may already be on your waiting list." I stand up and extend my hand to Kevin and then Paige. "It's always a pleasure doing business with you."

They shake hands with me, Montgomery, and Emerson. Then Paige and Drake leave us alone.

Montgomery turns backward, sits on the table, and swivels my laptop toward himself. He shuts all the pages I was just showing Paige and Kevin, opens several other pages, and starts tapping away on the device like he owns it.

"What's the status of that shipment of freeze-dried food on its way to Australia?" he asks. "The supplier better not have delayed again."

"No, they didn't. They sent me an email earlier to say the shipment is en route and the ship has left the port."

"That doesn't mean anything. How do we know they're telling the truth?"

"Look. They sent a satellite tracking code." I pivot over next to him, open my email inbox, and show him the satellite feed of the ship motoring across the Atlantic Ocean.

He snorts. "It's not even out of US territorial waters. The chumps must have only sent it today after we kicked them in the ass five times already. We'll never do business with that supplier again."

"I need you to go back upstairs and handle the medical supply order for the Irish Ranger Wing, Montgomery," I tell him. "I need you to double-check the inventory and make sure the supplier put the whole consignment on one cargo plane instead of four the way they did last time."

He scowls at me. "Where are you going?"

"I have to go to that college scholarship award ceremony. Don't you remember? I told you about it weeks ago. I even had your assistant put it on your calendar so you would know I would be out of the office today." I turn to Emerson. "You remember, don't you, Emerson?"

"Yes, Sir," Emerson replies. "I remember it very well."

"Of course you do. You would never forget a detail like that." I wave back and forth between them. "I'm sure you can run the office for a few hours without me. I'll be back later."

I leave and go to the scholarship awards. I go through the whole ceremony until it's time to leave.

I spend the last half hour shaking hands with five young black boys who have all just received college scholarships to attend whatever institute of higher education they've gotten into after graduating from high school.

They've all gotten into either Ivy League schools or other prestigious colleges in the Atlantic states area. The boys all beam with pride, relief, and happiness. Two of the boys wipe away tears.

Their families keep hugging them, telling the boys how proud the families are, and almost everyone in the five families cries their eyes out. Even the fathers cry. The fathers cry the most.

The families keep coming over to hug me, thank me, and gush on and on about their humble beginnings. I finally pry myself away, get into my limo, and my driver drives me back to the Halcyon Commercial Holdings office building.

I walk in feeling pretty damn good about life. My business is thriving. I'm founding charitable scholarships for underprivileged youth to attend the best schools in the country. Life can't get any better than this.

I stroll through the shipping pool on my way to my office. I'll check in with Montgomery and maybe go out to see a show tonight.

"How's the Irish Ranger Wing order coming?" I ask one of the dispatch clerks. "Did you get a cargo plane big enough to carry the whole order?

He looks up. "Excuse me, Sir?"

"The Irish Ranger Wing order." I stop dead in my tracks. "Didn't Montgomery ask you to follow it up?"

The clerk frowns at me. "Sir? I haven't spoken to Montgomery all day. He was out of the office the last I heard."

My blood boils. Montgomery's notoriously bad memory better not have interfered with this order. Emerson should have reminded his father to follow it up. This isn't like them at all.

I storm upstairs ready to break someone's balls. "Where's Montgomery?" I snap at his assistant once I get up to the executive level.

She blinks at me. "Sir? He's in his office as far as I know."

He better not be in his office and he better not be out of the office. He better not be anywhere other than downstairs in the shipping pool following up on the Irish Ranger Wing order—which I already know he isn't.

I storm into his office and actually scream out in horror. Montgomery lies on the floor staring up at the ceiling with a million stab wounds in his chest. Blood saturates his clothes, his hair, the carpet underneath him, and bubbles out of his mouth.

He's still trying to breathe. Blood erupts from his mouth and spatters everywhere every time he chokes on his own blood.

"MONTGOMERY!!" I dive for him, drop on my knees next to him, and fumble to start doing compressions.

A million things come into my mind in the first rush of panic. I should check his pulse. There is no way on God's green Earth I'm going to give him mouth-to-mouth with all that blood in the way. Hell no.

Part of my brain realizes that I shouldn't be doing CPR on him when I haven't checked a pulse and he is still breathing—if I can even call it that.

I also realize I shouldn't be doing CPR when he has all these stab wounds. They cover his chest, stomach, and even his sides. Doing CPR will only pump the blood out of him faster.

I can't stop myself from at least starting my pathetic version of compressions. I can't think at all. My body goes through the motions automatically.

I hear people screaming back and forth outside the office. I don't even care that I'm getting blood all over one of my best suits. I'll have to throw it away and replace it, but what the hell do I care? My business partner is bleeding to death right in front of me.

His eyes roll all over the office without seeing anything. He raises his hands off the floor, moves them around, and bumps them into me without actually doing anything. He can't make eye contact and his movements are too weak for him to know what he's doing.

"Hold on, Montgomery!" I whimper. "Please hold on....just hold on!"

I can barely breathe....and then someone pulls me away from him. "Mr. Espinosa!" someone yells in my ear. "Mr. Espinosa! You have to back off! The medics are here!"

I don't even see who it is that pulls me away. Someone else from the office yanks me to my feet and I stumble backward just as the paramedics flood the room.

Ian Nesbit, our company CTO, steers me far enough away that I can't see Montgomery anymore. I can't see what the medics are doing to him in there.

Ian stops me farther down the executive floor. He turns to face me—and his eyes dip to my suit. I'm covered in Montgomery's blood. This is a nightmare.

Ian's eyes go wide. He opens his mouth to speak, but no sound comes out. I feel myself shaking. I can't even move.

At least he doesn't leave me alone. I'm still standing there with him right in front of me when we hear someone yell, "Stand clear! Everybody clear? Shocking now!"

I can't listen to this. The thump in the background makes me sick to my stomach. I turn away, but I can't go anywhere—not like this.

The medics deliver four more shocks and then the sound changes in there. Someone else comes toward me.

"Mr. Espinosa?" a man asks. It's one of the medics. "Mr. Sinclair was just declared dead at the scene. The Police are on their way. I would ask you to stay here and not go anywhere or do anything until they get here."

Chapter 2:
Jocelyn

I get out of the elevator of Halcyon Commercial Holdings and find the executive floor already flooded with Police officers and crime scene people. "What do we got?" I ask one of the uniformed officers standing closest to the elevator.

"One of the company execs stabbed multiple times in his office." The officer points behind me. "The victim is in there. The guy who found him is over there covered in blood." The officer raises his eyebrows at me. "Diego Espinosa. He's a member of The Billionaires' Club."

The officer makes a few more suggestive faces at me like Diego belonging to The Billionaires' Club automatically makes him a murderer.

I glance back and forth around the executive floor. Too many crime scene people pack the victim's office. I would have to use a crowbar to fight my way in.

Diego stands off to one side covered in blood from his curly black hair all the way down to his polished black leather shoes. He's wearing what would be an extremely expensive suit if it wasn't completely saturated in blood.

Blood splatters his face and drenches his hands and neck. He keeps squirming like he wants to go clean himself up, but he can't.

Two other uniformed officers and two plain-clothes detectives stand there questioning him. Why am I even here if other members of the Force are already taking his statement?

I already know who Diego Espinosa is. He's Spanish, thirty-seven years old, and he isn't that tall or imposing. He has classic, almost Gypsy features and an extremely square jawline.

He doesn't have a reputation for being a player or a hothead or a vicious shark or any of the other things people say about members of The Billionaires' Club.

In fact, I honestly can't remember ever reading a negative word about him anywhere. I guess some of the members are dirtbags and some might actually be decent people. Anything is possible.

Some of the crime scene people come out of the victim's office just then, so I go in to check out the victim. He's an older, distinguished gentleman with white hair and a lined, weathered face.

He has a good build. He takes care of himself—or he did. I flag down one of the crime scene technicians. "Anything?" I ask.

The guy flips through his notes. "Fifty-nine-year-old Caucasian male, no known medical ailments, considered fit and healthy by his associates, stabbed fifteen times in the torso from three different angles—right, left, and center."

"No kidding! The killer certainly did a thorough job, didn't he?"

"The victim was found by Mr. Espinosa at two-twenty-five in the afternoon, commenced CPR at two-twenty-six....."

"Hold up," I interrupt. "He did CPR?"

"Yep. He did it for almost twenty minutes between when he found the victim and when emergency services showed up. One of his fellow execs pulled him away and the emergency services team declared Mr.

Sinclair dead at the scene at two-forty-seven." The guy looks up at me. "I'm thinking the victim died of blood loss, but that's just a wild-ass guess."

I laugh at his joke. "Good one, Robby."

More crime lab people leave. That gives me more space to look around the room. The crime lab people are already going over the entire place dusting for prints. They've already taken a million pictures and they're getting ready to remove the body.

Uniformed officers start taping off the executive floor. That doesn't leave me much to work with, so I go back out and intercept Diego while the other officers are still questioning him.

"I'm telling you my fingerprints will already be all over Montgomery's office." He speaks in a heavy Spanish accent. "I was in and out of that office all day every day! He was my business partner! I had no reason to kill him!"

"When did you say you left the building?" one of the plain-clothes detectives asks.

"I already told you." Diego groans and raises his hand like he wants to rub his eyes, but he stops himself in time. "I left at twelve-forty. I had to go uptown for a scholarship award ceremony at one. I left there at two and came straight back to the office. I even gave a speech at the ceremony. Five hundred people must have seen me there—and other people can vouch for my whereabouts in between times. I was hardly alone from one time to another—and everyone on the executive floor saw me go into Montgomery's office when I got back. They all saw me doing CPR."

I take out my notebook and start jotting down notes. It sounds to me like Diego has an iron-clad alibi for the time of the murder.

"When was the last time you saw Mr. Sinclair alive?" the same detective asks.

"I've already told you all of this!" Diego counters. "Why do you keep asking the same questions over and over again? I saw Montgomery alive during our meeting with Paige Novak and Kevin Drake—and the three of us stayed behind after Paige and Kevin left."

"What three of us?" the detective asks.

Diego groans and rolls his eyes. "I told you already! Montgomery, his son Emerson, and I met with Paige and Kevin. Paige and Kevin left at twelve-thirty. Montgomery, Emerson, and I stayed behind in the conference room and talked about our other business dealings until I left ten minutes later. That was the last time I saw Montgomery alive. You can ask Emerson. He was standing right there the whole time."

"What were you meeting with Mr. Drake and Ms. Novak about?" the detective asks.

"I already told you," Diego growls. "We were meeting about supplying medical equipment to different countries including the Russian and Chinese militaries."

"Isn't that against the law?" one of the uniformed officers asks.

Diego sneers at him. "It's medical equipment, Officer. It isn't military hardware. The equipment is designed to treat chronic conditions and genetic defects. It isn't used in combat situations or in any other military capacity. I'm quite sure the transactions are perfectly legal."

I've heard enough. I step forward. "Mr. Espinosa? My name is Jocelyn Hitchcock. I'm a detective with the NYPD."

He makes a face and dips his eyes to my badge. "I can read English, Detective. Thank you very much."

"I understand this is a frustrating process, but we need to ask you to come downtown with us."

He spins around. "Why? I can't be a suspect in this case. I wasn't alone with the victim during the time he was stabbed."

"Would you please just come downtown with us?" I repeat.

"Am I under arrest?"

"What would you do if I said yes?"

"If you say no, I won't go with you. I'm aware of the laws in this country, Ms......" He frowns at me and then at my badge. "Hitchcock? You're Asian."

Three other uniformed Police officers come over to us just then. They flank Diego and push me out of the way. "Diego Espinosa?" one of the officers asks. "You're under arrest for the murder of Montgomery Sinclair."

Two of the officers take hold of his arms, pull them behind his back, and the third officer starts cuffing Diego. He struggles.

"You can't do this! I'm innocent! I didn't kill Montgomery! I had no means, opportunity, or motive! I have an alibi! You can't do this!"

One of the uniformed officers starts reading Diego his Miranda warning. Diego protests through the whole thing and then they march him out of the building.

I drive back to the station with two other detectives. We spend half an hour going over the evidence and timeline for the murder. Then we all go downstairs to listen in on a few other detectives interviewing Diego again.

I stand behind the interrogation room's one-way mirror. Two uniformed officers stand guard on either side of him while he keeps repeating the same story over and over again.

"He certainly is consistent about it," my partner Beau Herstead remarks. "He hasn't changed his story even once."

"He's a scumbag," Detective Bonnie Larson snarls. "These rich cocksuckers don't give a shit who they kill as long as they get what they want."

Diego sits in the chair with his cuffed wrists behind him. He no longer protests his innocence nor does he get annoyed when the detectives ask him the same question more than once.

He stares at the tabletop in front of him and answers every question again and again in a dull, lifeless undertone. He repeats the same phrases no matter how many times the detectives ask. Diego doesn't even look up to make eye contact with them.

He goes through it all for an hour until one of the detectives asks for the millionth time what Diego and Montgomery Sinclair were talking about between the time Paige Novak and Kevin Drake left the conference room and when Diego left the conference room.

His dark eyes shoot up and lock on the detective directly across the table from him. "I want my phone call," Diego mutters. "I'm not going to answer any more questions until I get my phone call."

The detectives leave him alone and come into the observation room to consult with Sergeant Adam Kolter. He's the sergeant in charge of this case.

"He's been more than cooperative," a detective named Ruben Pickett points out. "He was cooperative the whole time we were at the scene."

"Give him his phone call and then transfer him down to the cells," the sergeant replies. "We got better things to do than keep listening to him say his Rosary all night long."

Ruben goes back into the room and gives Diego one of the cellphones registered to the NYPD. The department's computer system will automatically trace the call as soon as Diego makes it.

The uniformed officers uncuff him. He takes the phone and makes a very short, murmured conversation that none of us can overhear.

Beau checks something on the observation room computer. "The number is registered to a Jackson Metcalf of Metcalf Mining Industries. He's another member of The Billionaires' Club."

Diego only stays on the line for about a minute before he hangs up. He puts the phone on the table and goes back to staring at the tabletop.

The uniformed officers don't re-cuff Diego. He looks so defeated that they don't have to. They escort him out of the room.

The rest of us go back to what we were doing, but only for fifteen minutes before a bunch of strangers come into the station. The sergeant gets a phone call to let him know that Diego's lawyer is downstairs demanding to see him.

Sergeant Kolter takes me, Bonnie, Ruben, and Beau downstairs to meet up with the lawyer so we can be present when he sees Diego.

We get a surprise when we meet up with six men instead of one. An older, square-shouldered gentleman with white hair holds out his hand to Sergeant Kolter. Everyone knows this man. He's Dante Helme.

Jackson Metcalf and Kevin Drake come with him. Dante introduces the other three as The Billionaires' Club's criminal defense team.

"These three men will be defending Diego against any legal action the city decides to take against him," Dante informs us. "He told us he's already under arrest, so you'll need to make your evidence available to his defense team."

"We haven't finished questioning him yet," Sergeant Kolter tells him. "Once we finish that...."

"Yes, you have finished questioning him." One of the lawyers pulls a sheaf of paper out of his leather case and hands it over. "This is an injunction signed by Judge Millhouse prohibiting you from questioning the suspect any further, striking all his previous statements from the record as illegally obtained, and ordering you to release Mr. Espinosa immediately. Any delay will be considered unlawful imprisonment and wrongful arrest." The guy pretends to check his watch. "You have five minutes to turn him over to us or I'll be calling in the NYPD to arrest you, Sergeant. I suggest you hurry along downstairs and release Mr. Espinosa immediately."

Sergeant Kolter stiffens—and then his eyes dip to the paperwork in front of him. He doesn't even have time to read it before his five minutes run out.

He walks off leaving the four of us detectives standing there with our fingers up our noses. The three billionaires and the three lawyers stare straight back at us. None of them even flinches.

These guys certainly brought out the big guns. They must be able to pull some pretty heavy-weight strings if they got a court order for Diego's release in less than fifteen minutes. I'm impressed.

Sergeant Kolter comes back with Diego. He still looks awful. He starts to get emotional when the three billionaires pull him into their group. They pat him on the back and Jackson even squeezes the back of Diego's neck in a comforting way.

They all murmur in his ear to encourage him and he nods. "You won't be able to leave the area, Mr. Espinosa," Sergeant Kolter tells him. "We may need to call you in to further clarify your statement."

"My client won't be coming in again nor will he be answering any further questions or clarifying anything," the same lawyer guy returns.

All seven of them turn away to leave the station, but not before we hear the same lawyer tell Diego and the other three billionaires not to talk to the Police at all.

Chapter 3: Diego

"I'm telling you I had nothing to do with this!" I blurt out as soon as I get outside the Police station. "I told them a million times."

"For someone who understands the law as well as you do, you should have known better than to say a word to the Police," one of the lawyers tells me.

His name is Kieran Speight. The other two are Garrett Trask and Mose Fuchs. They all work for the same legal firm that represents The Billionaires' Club.

One of the club's functions is to provide legal assistance to any member who needs it, especially in cases where someone gets accused of a crime merely because they happen to be a member of the club.

Night has fallen while I've been getting interrogated by the Police. I've been here all afternoon and evening.

Kieran's comments make me wilt. "I know," I mumble. "I just reacted in the moment. I just wanted to explain....I messed up."

"It doesn't matter because nothing you said will count against you in the unlikely event that this case ever goes to court," he replies. "All your statements will be stricken from the record."

"I don't want them to be stricken from the record!" I tell him. "I didn't do anything wrong! I did not kill Montgomery!"

"We know you didn't," Kevin replies. "We know you better than to think that."

"Well, *they* obviously do!" I wave toward the station. "I have to beat this! An accusation like this could ruin me even if I am innocent!"

"That's our job, Mr. Espinosa," Kieran tells me. "Now I think you better go home and get cleaned up—and don't talk to anyone about this case—or anything else."

"I have to conduct my business, Kieran! I will have to talk to some people. I'm sorry."

He only smiles at me. "Of course. I didn't mean that."

I snort at him. I don't remind him that he did actually just say not to talk to anyone about literally anything.

Jackson pulls me away. "Come on, man. I'll drive you home."

The three lawyers walk off in the other direction. Dante and Kevin accompany me and Jackson to Jackson's big black Range Rover. He opens the back, pulls out a towel, and drapes it over the passenger seat to protect it from my bloody clothes.

Kevin grips my shoulder again. None of these men hesitate to touch me even if it means getting blood on their hands. They don't even seem to notice how dirty I am except that they want to help me get cleaned up.

"I won't tell you not to worry about this, but just remember that we're all behind you," Kevin tells me. "None of us will stop doing business with you because of this. We all know you had no reason to kill Montgomery."

"Of course I didn't! He was my business partner!"

"Go home and get cleaned up, man," Dante tells me. "You look awful. I'm sure you'll feel better once you take a shower and change your clothes. One of us can stay with you if you don't want to be alone."

I turn away, but that only brings me face to Jackson's vehicle. "I need to be alone. I need to think about this before I face the world."

"Whatever you need," Dante murmurs. "You have all our numbers. Don't hesitate to call one of us no matter what it is or what time of the day or night."

I'm too grateful for their help and support. "Thank you," I mumble. "All of you. You're the best friends a man could have."

"Go on home," Kevin tells me. "Why don't I come see you in your office tomorrow? We can talk about our businesses and I can take a look around and see if you need help with anything. I'm sure you'll need some extra people, now that Montgomery won't be around."

I can only nod. "Thank you, Kevin. I would really appreciate that."

He pats me on the back again and gives me a subtle push toward the passenger door. Jackson stands there holding it open for me to get in.

I can't even look at my friends when I sit down in the seat. Jackson lays another towel over me to protect the seatbelt from all the blood. I don't even care that he's protecting his car. The care these men are taking of me makes me want to cry. At least someone cares.

He exchanges a few words with Dante and Kevin on the sidewalk before Jackson gets into the driver's seat and motors away into the night. He doesn't say a word all the way to my house.

I live in a big mansion on the Upper East Side. It occupies most of a city block behind a high brick wall covered in ivy. Jackson stops at the gate and rolls down his window to talk to the security guard.

"Oh, good evening, Mr. Metcalf," the guard exclaims and shoots me a glance. "Is everything all right?"

"I hope so, Benny. I'm just dropping off Mr. Espinosa. I'll be out of your hair in a few minutes."

"Take your time, Sir," the guard replies. "Thank you for your help."

The guard opens the gate and Jackson pulls into the big circular driveway in front of the grand house entrance doors. A fountain surrounded by flowers occupies the middle of the driveway.

Jackson gets out, opens the passenger door for me, and takes the top towel away after I unbuckle my seatbelt.

He faces me in the dark outside the car once I get out and straighten up. "Are you sure you don't want me to stick around?" he asks. "It's no trouble—really. I don't like leaving you alone."

"I'll be fine, Jackson," I murmur. "Thank you for your help—and thank you for your offer. Believe me, I'm extremely grateful for your care and attention. I need to be alone right now. I would feel like I had to pay attention to you and offer you hospitality if you stayed. I know you don't mean it that way, but please just go home. I'll be fine. I need time to myself to think."

"Okay, brother." He actually comes forward and gives me a hug. I can't tell in the darkness if he gets blood on his clothes. He doesn't seem to notice one way or the other. "It's a huge honor for me that I'm the one you called tonight. I want to be the one you call if you need anything—and I mean anything. I understand why you need tonight to yourself, but don't go through this alone. Lean on your friends. That's what we're here for."

I can only nod down at the ground and thank him again. He won't leave until I go first, so I walk off into the house. He gets in his car and drives away into the night.

He has a wife and children at home—and he's out here helping me. I couldn't in good conscience let him stay here babysitting me. That wouldn't be right.

I don't wake up any of the servants. I go straight to my own apartment and get into the shower before I take my clothes off.

I strip completely naked and dump everything right there in the shower before I step back out in my bare feet. My feet are the one part of me that is still relatively clean.

I wash my hands in the bathroom sink first. My suit jacket and shirt protected my arms above the wrists, so I only have to wash my hands that far. I take off my watch and wash that, too. It's waterproof, so I don't have to worry about damaging it.

I leave it on the sink vanity and walk down the corridor to one of the housekeeper's supply closets. No one sees me walking around the house naked. Everyone is asleep. I'm the only one moving around.

I take a large black plastic garbage bag from the closet, return to my room, and put all my ruined clothes in the bag. Then I take the longest, hottest, soapiest shower of my life.

A lot of blood comes out of my hair, but most of it soaked into my clothes. Dante is right. I feel much better once I get cleaned off, dry myself, and put on clean clothes.

It's already midnight, so I get into bed. I thought when I left the station that I would be too worried about this to sleep, but exhaustion and the heat from the shower calm me down enough.

I crash and wake up at seven the next morning. I always wake up at seven no matter what else I'm doing or how much sleep I've gotten.

I put on a new suit and go to the dining room to eat breakfast. I'm in the middle of checking the news when I get a phone call from Ian Nesbit.

"Where are you, man?" he practically shrieks. "The whole damn company is melting down!"

"What are you talking about, Ian? I'm at home eating breakfast exactly the same way I do every morning—and what do you mean the company is melting down? How could it possibly melt down in less than twenty-four hours?"

"The Police cordoned off the executive floor and now none of the executives know what the hell to do! The Irish Ranger Wing is up our asses over their order and the satellite link lost contact with the Australia order....."

I groan and put down my fork. "Fine, Ian. I'm on my way right now. I'll straighten it out."

I hang up on him, call my car, and ride to the office. Montgomery was notoriously forgetful about monitoring our ongoing deals—and now the whole company falls apart the minute he's gone. Great.

Chapter 4: Diego

I show up to work and walk into a scene of utter chaos, panic, and mass confusion. The executives who usually remain hermetically sealed in the building's upper floors now run amok all over the building amongst the rank and file.

The executives keep giving contradictory orders to everyone and arguing about what to do and who is making the wrong decision about what while the regular workers stand around waiting for someone to tell them what to do.

I see the problem right away and point at Ian and the other executives. "All of you go upstairs..."

"We can't go upstairs," Ian interrupts. "The executive floor is off limits until the Police finish the investigation."

"I know that, Ian," I snap. "All of you go upstairs to the north corner conference room and stay there. I want all of you to turn your phones to *Do Not Disturb* until I come up there and tell you to turn them back on. Is that clear?"

The executives exchange glances. One man's death can't possibly cause this kind of pandemonium. I'll never believe that.

I wait for the executives to get into the elevator and the doors close. Then I turn to the nearest dispatch clerk.

"Get on the phone and get me the biggest cargo plane you can find. I don't care where the plane is in the world. I don't care how much you have to pay for it. Just get it and send it to JFK on the double. Understand?"

He nods fast and attacks his computer. I go down the line to the next clerk. This one is a woman.

"I want you to contact the supplier for the Irish Ranger Wing order and get the shipment on the trucks and en route to JFK within the hour. Inform the supplier that, if the shipment isn't on the trucks, on the road, and en route within the hour, they'll be hearing from our legal team with a civil suit for breach of contract—and I'll be seeking in the hundreds of millions for punitive damages. Is that clear?"

She squeaks, "Yes, Sir," and jumps on her computer, too.

I go from one clerk to another putting out fires until I come to the last computer. "Pull up the satellite link for the Australia order," I tell the clerk.

He pulls it up and I stare at the feed. A giant gale-force storm is blocking the feed of the ship, but the storm is already moving away toward the west. The ship's route will bring it out the other side of the storm on the way down the west coast of Africa.

"Should we do anything about it, Sir?" the clerk asks.

"Do anything about it like what—divert a gale force storm? Don't do anything. I'll contact the Australian government about the delay in the shipment and claim force majeure. That's the best we can do."

I walk away and head for the elevator. I'm on my way upstairs to deal with those kindergarteners known as my executive team when I get sidetracked by the IT team. The computer system is suffering from some kind of virus.

"I'm on my way upstairs to talk to the executives," I tell the technician who reports the problem. "I'll send Ian down to straighten it out."

I make it up to the conference room to find half the executives pacing the room and the other half sitting in their chairs and clasping their hands in pensive tension like they're all waiting for the Last Judgement of Doomsday.

I walk over to Ian and hold out my hand. "Give me your phone."

He hands it over.

"Go downstairs to the IT department and help your subordinates straighten out whatever virus is clogging up the system," I tell him.

He frowns. "What virus?"

"I'm sure they'll tell you when you get down there. Now go, Ian. Don't leave the department until you clean it up and get the system running again. Then you can come and report to me."

He leaves, thank God. I turn to the other execs. First I start with Kendrick Blakely, our exec in charge of personnel. I tell him to go down to the IT department, too, and bring up a new laptop for every member of the executive team.

Then I go through the entire floor of the building. This floor has multiple spare offices we use for meetings and such.

I assign each of the executives a new office, give them each a new laptop, and tell them they can turn on their phones and start doing their jobs from here exactly the same way they did their jobs upstairs.

Honestly, why am I the only person who thought of that? Why am I walking around holding these people's hands when they're the ones who are supposed to be running the company?

Each of them relaxes in relief as soon as I tell them what to do. Jesus Christmas, what is the world coming to?

I'm just on my way downstairs to show Ian where he can start setting up his new office. I get out of the elevator on the IT floor and meet up with Kevin coming out of the stairwell.

"Hello," he greets me. "One of the dispatch clerks told me where to find you."

I groan and roll my eyes at him. "Don't ever become a CEO, Kevin. I mean it."

He laughs. "It's too late, man. I already am one." He claps me on the shoulder. "You look much better this morning. We were all really worried about you last night."

"You should have been worried about this company."

I walk into the IT department. I tell Ian where to go, give him his phone back, and send him on his way.

Kevin stands off to one side watching until I finish. "Are you seriously telling me none of them even thought to use another floor for their offices?"

I make a face at him. "Who knew Montgomery was such an essential cog in the machinery." I find myself looking around. "I wonder where Emerson is."

"I'm sure he's destroyed by his father's death," Kevin replies. "Do you want me to find out? I could track him down."

"No, leave him alone. I'm sure you're right. Getting news like that would mess anyone up."

"So what do you want me to do here?" he asks. "You look like you have it under control."

I'm just about to tell him that I do when all the lights in the building go down. They plunge us into darkness. "Forget I asked," Kevin tells me in the dark.

"Come on. Let's go find the maintenance department."

We grope our way into the stairwell and hold onto the rails until we climb all the way down to the basement where the maintenance crewmen live in their holes.

We find the maintenance team walking around with flashlights. "What the hell is going on down here?" I demand. "Why aren't you turning the power back on?"

"We can't," the maintenance boss tells me. "The system is computer controlled. It must be a network problem. You should check with the IT department."

"I don't believe it," I growl and turn to Kevin. "Will you please go upstairs and make sure none of the executives jump out of the window or something?"

He laughs again. "Sure, man. Anything else?"

"Yes. I'm going to send you some phone numbers and instructions to give people on the other end. I need to keep some of my fulfillment channels open until we straighten this out."

He leaves and I go to the IT department to crack a few heads. I spend the rest of the day going from one disaster to another. There is no possible way so much can go wrong so quickly at the worst possible time.

Kevin even calls in Niko Holloway to help straighten out some of Halcyon's transit issues.

"I should have been using Niko all along," I mutter to Kevin at the end of the day. "We never would have had this problem if we used him. I definitely learned my lesson today. I won't make that mistake again."

"We're having a club meeting tomorrow," he tells me. "You should come. It will help take your mind off of everything and get you out of the office for a few hours at least."

"That's what I'm worried about."

He only grins. "Just come. Don't hide in a corner dwelling on it. Try to get your life back to normal as much as possible. We all want to support you. At least you'll be able to relax at the club and know that everyone there is on your side and not out to get you."

Chapter 5: Jocelyn

I get out of my car and flash my badge at the security guards. A skinny young white kid holds up his hand to me. "Just wait a minute, Ma'am. Just let me call upstairs and find out about this before we let you in."

I wait while he gets on his phone and makes a phone call. "Yes, Sir, it's Ricky. I'm down here at the door and an NYPD detective just showed up and wants to come inside. Yes, Sir. Yes, Sir, I understand." He hangs up and turns to me. "Someone will be right down to talk to you."

I wait on the sidewalk until two men come out. One of them is Kevin Drake. The other is a much younger, much darker, and much more formidable character.

Kevin holds out his hand to me. "I'm Kevin Drake."

"I know who you are, Mr. Drake," I tell him. "I'm here investigating the Montgomery Sinclair murder. You can understand that we want to interview the closest business associates of both the victim and the main suspect."

"Yes, I understand that." Kevin waves to the man next to him. "This is Rory Kahn. He's our PR officer. He'll be the one showing you around, answering your questions, and liaising between you and the members."

"And I should add, Detective," Rory interjects, "that none of the members will answer questions about the murder or anything related to Mr. Sinclair's or Mr. Espinosa's activities. You can ask all the questions you want about the club and our associations with the two men, but we won't answer any questions directly related to this investigation. I'll escort you around the club and I'll intervene if I hear you ask any of the members anything they shouldn't be answering."

"I can appreciate that. Thank you for your cooperation in this matter."

Kevin leaves us alone. Rory escorts me inside. We walk through the entrance doors and up a flight of stairs to a big room full of tasteful furniture.

Twenty men stand around talking, eating from the buffet, helping themselves to drinks at the wet bar in the corner, playing pool, watching TV, or working on computers either together or alone.

Some of them just sit on the couch working on their phones, but the majority stand in clusters talking.

I stop at the top of the stairs, cast a quick look around, and spot Diego on the opposite side of the room. He's talking to three other men. He has his back to me and doesn't turn around.

I don't know who to talk to first. All the men in the room wear expensive suits. They look like stockbrokers.

Rory sees me hesitate and waves me toward the nearest cluster. The group includes Dante Helme, Jackson Metcalf, and Kevin Drake as well as Lane Prince, Derek Salazar, and Giovanni Nowaczyk.

"Dante is our current club president," Rory tells me. "Jackson is our finance officer at the moment. Kevin has been our membership officer for years. He handles new applicants and any other matters related to the club's membership. Judah Hayes is our events officer. He isn't here right now, but I'm sure the rest of us can answer your questions as well as he can."

"How long has Diego been a member of the club?" I ask.

"Seven years," Kevin tells me. "He had been living in New York for quite a few years before he qualified to join."

"Does the club have a citizenship requirement?" I ask. "Can anyone join regardless of their nationality?"

"We don't have a citizenship requirement. Nationality doesn't enter the picture. We don't even have a requirement that the person lives in New York or even on the Eastern Seaboard. We would take anyone with a billion-dollar net worth no matter where they lived or worked in the world, but we're mostly interested in people who operate locally. Networking and business connections are a big part of what we do, so it's important to us that we see the person regularly. We want to support them and for them to support us in all our endeavors, both professionally and personally." He hesitates for a second. "And Diego is a citizen, by the way. I'm not sure if you knew that. He has dual US and Spanish citizenship, so it wouldn't be an issue for him even if we did have a policy about it."

I raise my eyebrows. "I did not know that. Thank you for telling me."

"Diego is a good man," Jackson interjects. "He cares about people. He takes care of his employees and associates and he takes care of society."

"What do you mean—he takes care of society?" I ask.

"He contributes," Dante explains. "He uses his money to help others. He sets up scholarship funds, charitable organizations, education programs, and afterschool activity programs to help people in need and to keep kids out of gangs and prison."

"The day Montgomery died, Diego attended an awards ceremony granting five scholarships to graduating high school boys from Harlem," Rory tells me. "That's where he was right before he returned to the office and found Montgomery dead. Didn't you know that? Diego was the one who set up the scholarship fund for those boys. You should talk to their families about what kind of man Diego is."

I try not to make a face. "I'm sure bad people are just as capable of setting up scholarship funds as good people."

"It isn't just the scholarship fund," Lane interjects. "He's one of the most charitable members of the club—even more than the rest of us."

I glance around the group. "Do you all contribute charitably?"

"Of course," Kevin replies. "What's the point of having money if you don't do some good with it?"

"And don't get me started on all the jobs he's created in his companies and the internal contributions he makes to his employees," Dante adds. "He buys Christmas and birthday presents for all his employees, their wives, husbands, and children. He keeps a catalogue of their birthdays, so he's giving out gifts practically all year round. He's even sent some of his employees' kids to college or overseas on trips. He sent one of his employees' high-school-age daughter to London so she could take part in a Shakespeare competition at the Globe Theater."

"He does shit like that all the time," Giovanni chimes in. "He does it so often it's sometimes easy to forget that he's doing it at all."

"Did Montgomery Sinclair contribute charitably?" I ask.

"I wouldn't know that," Lane replies. "I didn't do business with Montgomery."

"Was there a reason for that?"

"Yes, there was a reason." He stares straight back at me and doesn't look away.

I wait for him to say something else before I ask, "What was the reason?"

"It came out a few years ago that I had a criminal record and had served time before I got out and went into business for myself. Montgomery was on good terms with me before that, but he stopped doing business with me then. He barely spoke to me in public at all after that unless it was absolutely necessary. I got the message loud and clear and he never approached me about doing business ever again. So I never approached him and we never did do business again."

"Wow. That sounds like a hostile situation."

"It wasn't hostile. He made a decision to distance himself from me and I let him. He wasn't the only one."

"Did Diego ever do anything like that—to any of you?"

"Of course not," Lane counters. "Diego was one of the few who supported me."

"Every member of this club has a story like that," Rory interjects. "Diego is the salt of the earth. He would never let a little thing like that get in the way of genuinely treating people with the respect and dignity they deserve. He's one of the most caring men in the club."

"And I don't believe for a second that he killed Montgomery," Lane goes on. "Or anyone else for that matter. I will never believe that if I live a million years."

"I don't believe it, either," Jackson adds. "I could believe it of a lot of other people, but not him."

My eye skips from one face to another. The men around me all return my gaze without a flicker of hesitation.

I am definitely going to have to look into these reports about The Billionaires' Club members making charitable donations and helping out their employees. I've never heard of that. I've only ever heard of billionaires being rapacious, money-grubbing scumbags.

I turn to Kevin. "I understand that you and Paige Novak where in the room with Diego, Montgomery, and Montgomery's son Emerson right up until Montgomery was last seen alive."

"That's correct. We were."

"Diego claims you were there doing business with him and Montgomery about some sale of equipment to the Russian military."

"That's also correct. It's medical equipment. It isn't military hardware or anything like that. My company supplies trained personnel to use the equipment as well as the training itself when a military wants to use their own people."

"Can you tell me anything about the meeting? Did you notice anything unusual about the interaction between Mr. Espinosa and Mr. Sinclair?"

"There was nothing unusual about it. It was the most ordinary, unremarkable meeting in history. We met. We talked. We left. There was nothing going on between them that hasn't been going on the whole time we've been in business with them."

"Do you know if there was any conflict going on between Diego and Montgomery—either something business-related or personal?"

"There was never any conflict between Diego and Montgomery," Kevin tells me. "They got along well and did business together for years."

"Except that Montgomery had a terrible memory," Dante interjects. "He was extremely forgetful. That was pretty much the only thing about him that annoyed Diego. Other than that, they were the best of friends."

Chapter 6: Diego

I pace from one computer to another, bend over the dispatch clerks' screens, and read what they're doing. I have to check again and again and correct errors and problems as they pop up.

I hate to admit it, but Montgomery had his fingers in a lot more pies than I realized. He really was integral to my business and handled a lot of things I didn't realize he was handling behind the scenes.

Now things are falling apart without him—or they would be if I wasn't here to pick up the slack.

I'm in the middle of straightening out another legal apocalypse with two of my other suppliers when a hush falls over the shipping pool. I look up and see Emerson Sinclair standing in the doorway. He looks completely wrecked.

He barely looks up to make eye contact with anyone. He's dressed in one of his stylish suits with his hair perfectly combed and his face freshly shaved, but I've never seen him so devastated. He struggles to control his features.

I go over to him and grip both his shoulders. "You don't have to be here if you don't want to be," I murmur. "We'll handle the business if you need to take time to yourself."

"I want to be here," he chokes. "I want to help...you....and the other execs. I can't.....I don't know what to do....."

"Come here."

I lead him to a side office where the dispatch manager usually works. I park Emerson behind the desk and bring up the pages I've been working on with the clerks out in the pool.

"These are all our ongoing situations I'm dealing with right now," I tell him. "I need you to field emails from clients and suppliers and relay the information to the clerks out there. Understand? I need you to feed us a constant supply of updated information so I don't have to keep checking it. Do you understand?"

He nods without looking up. I don't feel right about him being here, but this must be what he needs.

He sits down in the manager's chair and starts clicking on the computer. I hesitate to leave him alone, but one of the clerks calls me out into the pool just then. I go back to what I'm doing. I'm sure I'll be the first to know if Emerson gets overwhelmed and wants to leave.

I work for an hour and still don't manage to dig my way out of the weeds before I get another phone call. This one is from the receptionist at the front entrance to the Halcyon building.

"There's a detective here from the NYPD who says she wants to look around and talk to some of the employees," the receptionist tells me.

I stiffen. "Let me guess. Is she a young Asian woman in casual clothes?"

"Yes, Sir. She says her name is Jocelyn Hitchcock."

I groan. Not her again. "Contact security and tell them to escort her around the building. Inform the security guard that she isn't allowed to ask anyone anything about the murder investigation. She can ask anything she wants about the company. If she starts asking about anything else, the security guard should escort her off the premises."

"Yes, Sir. I understand."

I hang up and call Kieran Speight. He tells me the same thing. Jocelyn can ask anything she wants about how the company works. He forbids me to answer any questions about the murder or my interactions with Montgomery.

I have a hard time concentrating after that. I go around the pool and warn everyone that Jocelyn is coming down. I also hold a quick conversation with Emerson to tell him the same thing about not answering any questions about the investigation.

He doesn't look up. "I understand," he mumbles. I would be surprised if Jocelyn could get anything out of him anyway.

It takes a while for her to work her way down to the shipping pool. I'm in the middle of checking the progress of the Australia shipment when she comes in with her security escort.

She's a petite woman of about thirty. She doesn't wear suits or any other kind of professional business wear, but she always looks put together. She has a way of coming across as casual even though she attends to every detail of her appearance.

This is the third time I've seen her in public and she always wears the same outfit. She wears tight black pants that hug her curves all the way down to her ankles. She wears a dark purple leather jacket cinched at the waist with a black T-shirt underneath.

She walks around on mid-level black leather ankle boots. Her outfit makes her look chic, timeless, and universal. She would look appropriate in a business setting or a casual setting no matter where it was.

She wears her hair in a half-up, half-down style with wisps surrounding her face and falling in front of her ears. She has a distinctly Asian look and at the same time she looks modern, cosmopolitan, and very American.

She doesn't speak with an accent, so she must have been born here. She has such an American surname. She may have a Caucasian father, but I don't see anything sign of mixed ancestry in her features.

I play off her arrival like it means nothing to me. I go to the other side of the pool while she goes around talking to the clerks one after the other.

I have plenty to do to keep up with our logistics while the clerks deal with her. I field phone calls from the executive team and answer more emails and other business on my phone.

I try to pretend not to hear what Jocelyn ask the clerks and what they say in return. They all defend me and tell her that they don't believe I could do anything wrong, especially not to Montgomery.

"Diego is the only one keeping the lights on," one of the clerks tells her. "He's the only reason we're still in business. All the employees would be out on the street without him."

Emerson keeps communicating with us and sending out relevant information to keep us updated, but he has to stop when she goes in there to talk to him.

I keep working on my phone and coordinating the clerks and every other aspect of the business, but I can't help listening in on her conversation with Emerson.

"Did your father get along with Diego?" she asks.

"My father loved Diego," Emerson murmurs. "My father thought the sun rose and set on Diego. Diego was his best friend."

"Do you know if Diego felt the same way?"

Emerson nods. "I'm certain he did. Diego treated my father like the brother he never had. I grew up around them and I never heard Diego say a harsh word to my father—ever. They were extremely close. They worked together every day and got along in everything. I don't believe Diego could ever do anything to harm my father—and Diego would never break the law, either. He's one of the most law-abiding men I've ever met—even more than my father was."

Jocelyn comes over to me next. I have a hard time facing her, but I force myself to do it. "Detective," I greet her.

"I appreciate you letting me interview your employees," she tells me. "I hope you understand that this is nothing personal and I'm just doing my job here."

"Yes, of course I understand that, Detective, and I hope that you will also understand that I am simply trying to protect myself and my business by seeking legal advice."

"Of course. I would expect nothing less and I promise I won't ask you anything about the murder."

"What can I do for you, then?"

She glances around the pool. "Can I ask what you're working on here?"

"As you can see, this is the shipping pool where we monitor delivery of our contractual goods from supplier to client. We've been having problems since Montgomery's death—problems that call for me to step in and handle things in ways I didn't have to before."

She raises her eyebrows. "What problems would those be?"

"Straightening out issues and wrinkles with the fulfilment of our contracts—unforeseen circumstances, computer problems, infrastructure failures—that sort of thing."

"So would Montgomery have handled those otherwise?"

"I wouldn't have thought so, but apparently he did. I'm thrust into this situation as a result." I notice something on the screen in front of me and tap the clerk on the shoulder. "You forgot the decimal point there."

I have to take a call on my phone from Ian. He still hasn't completely eliminated the virus from our system, which causes more problems.

I get distracted and Jocelyn leaves in the confusion. Thank Heaven she's gone. Life is hard enough without her around.

Chapter 7:
Jocelyn

I sit down at my desk and pull up everything I can find about Diego Espinosa. Kevin Drake is right. Diego has dual citizenship.

His American father held a diplomatic post in Spain, married a Spanish woman, and Diego and his two brothers and one sister grew up there. Diego's father registered Diego and his siblings as citizens born abroad, so Diego really is a citizen.

I also check up on his charities, scholarships, and youth programs. He has a lot more of them than even the other billionaires mentioned. That surprises me.

It surprises me even more now than it did when his friends mentioned it at the club. I don't know why it surprises me because I always kind of knew that the rich and famous donated to charities.

I guess I never realized before how extensive and pervasive the practice is amongst these people. Most of the billionaires in the club have their own pet charities they donate to, but Diego takes it to another level.

His tax returns for the last seven years indicate he's spent an ungodly amount of money gifting to his employees' personal lives. He's bought them cars and even homes in some cases.

He's sent quite a few of their children to college. That seems to be one of his favorite ways to help people out—either by sending them to college or sending their children to college if their parents can't afford it.

He's gotten kids out of jail, paid for them to get job training, and then taken them into his company to keep them off the streets.

He and Kevin Drake run a program in Harlem that intervenes the very first time a kid goes to juvenile hall.

Kevin and Diego pay the kid's legal fees, funnel them into a job training and professional development course run by Kevin's organization, and place them in a job for which the program trained them.

Kevin and Diego also have a fund to pay for any assistance and intervention the kid's family needs. The fund helps pay for the family's living expenses, debts, legal fees, medical costs, or anything else the kid might be trying to pay for by turning to crime.

Both Diego and Kevin are intimately involved in these young people's lives. Both Kevin and Diego regularly meet with the kids in the program to talk to them, find out what they need, and to get to know their personal problems.

I stare at my screen for a long time. Jackson is right about Diego. He really is a good man. He genuinely cares about people and he uses his money to give back. So why is he even the main suspect in this investigation?

I switch back over to the crime scene reports and Diego's statements about his whereabouts and activities leading up to finding Montgomery.

Diego has an alibi. Bonnie and Ruben have been interviewing people from the scholarship award ceremony. Diego really was there when he says he was there.

His limo driver reports that Diego never went anywhere else after leaving the Halcyon building and coming back after the ceremony. Every minute of that time is accounted for.

I can only find one or two brief snatches of time when he wasn't in a witness's direct line of sight. Those few minutes aren't enough for him to get back to the building in time to murder Montgomery.

We never should have arrested Diego in the first place—so why did we? The order came down from even higher than Sergeant Kolter. Did the department single out Diego because he's a member of The Billionaire's Club?

A bunch of other reports come in on the crime scene. The autopsy doesn't reveal anything we didn't already know.

Montgomery Sinclair was exceptionally healthy for his age, wasn't on any medications, and didn't suffer from any chronic or age-related medical problems.

The crime lab techs did find cocaine residue on his jacket, but there was no trace of cocaine or any other drug in his bloodstream.

The residue turned up on his jacket lapels. The results indicate that the killer had cocaine on his or her hands. Whoever it was appears to have grabbed Montgomery by the jacket in what could have been a scuffle leading to the victim's death.

Diego really does look innocent from where I'm sitting. What other possible reason could the department have to arrest him except to get the high-profile news story that they'd arrested a member of The Billionaires' Club for violently murdering his business partner?

This also explains why Diego did CPR on the victim. I might be able to believe that Diego staged the whole thing so he would be the one to find the victim and then make himself look innocent by doing CPR.

I don't think so, though. I've learned a few things about human nature in this job and my money is on Diego. Besides, his alibi is damn well bulletproof. I honestly don't see how he could possibly be the killer. He couldn't have gotten near the building in time.

I'm still going through the evidence when I get a phone call from Sergeant Kolter to report to him in his office. He keeps shuffling papers on his desk while we talk.

"How close are you to pinning the Sinclair murder on the billionaire?" he asks.

"That's the thing, Sarge. I don't think he did it. I've never seen such an airtight alibi. He was on the other side of town in front of five hundred witnesses when the victim was stabbed. Espinosa can't be the killer. I don't know why the department has it out for him...."

"Where's Beau?" Sergeant Kolter asks. "Maybe he found something."

"He still hasn't come back from interviewing all the witnesses who saw Espinosa at the awards ceremony—and we already have over two hundred statements confirming Espinosa's alibi. He's innocent, Sarge. We should drop the charges. He didn't do it."

"Of course he did it. He's a billionaire. He probably thinks he can use his money to get out of it." He goes back to what he was doing. "Just find the evidence. Find a way. You're smart like that. I know you can do it."

I leave his office. Stellar. Now I'm the one getting set up to frame an innocent man.

I go back to my desk and pull up Diego's criminal record—except that he doesn't have one. He's never been arrested for anything—ever. Montgomery doesn't have one, either.

Neither of them has any record of drug use or any shady business dealings. All their business is perfectly legitimate. They make certain of it even when they deal overseas.

I even check with Interpol. Diego isn't wanted for anything in Europe and has no record there, either, not even from when he was younger. He's completely clean.

Some of his youth intervention programs are specifically targeted to help kids avoid drug addiction and to get out of it if they do get hooked. He could be doing that to make up for the error of his younger ways.

Helping kids stay off drugs could mean anything, but I would tend to think it would show up on his record if he had been involved in it before.

The more obvious explanation is that he never got involved in it just like he never got involved in any other illegal activity. Now he wants to make sure other kids don't get involved in it, either.

Don't ask me how I'm supposed to cook anything up on the guy when there's nothing to cook up. This case looks pretty straightforward to me—at least where Diego is concerned.

Chapter 8: Diego

I walk into a conference room where Kieran Speight and Mose Fuchs are already waiting for me. We all shake hands.

"Don't say a single word to the cops," Kieran tells me. "Let us do all the talking."

"So you just want me to sit here in silence for the whole meeting?" I ask.

"Yes, exactly," Kieran replies. "Don't say one word. Don't even say hello to them."

I don't know what to say to that. It sounds awfully rude. I should be cooperating with the investigation to help the cops see that I'm innocent, but I'm not the lawyer here.

I don't have a chance to protest any further before Jocelyn comes in with her partner. He's a thick-set, burly, linebacker-type guy in a used suit. The identification card next to his badge reads, *Detective Beau Herstead.*

We all shake hands. I nod at Beau and Jocelyn, but I don't say hello. This will be the first time ever in my life I haven't greeted someone on meeting them in public. I guess there's a first time for everything, but my father would be scandalized.

The five of us sit down. Mose and Kieran sit on either side of me. Beau starts questioning me again about the timeline of me finding Montgomery's body.

"My client won't answer any questions about the murder," Kieran interrupts. "Was there something else you wanted to ask?"

"He has to answer questions about the murder. That's what we're here for." Beau turns to me. "You're only making it worse for yourself by withholding evidence."

"My client has cooperated with the investigation enough," Kieran fires back. "You're overstepping your authority by asking him to incriminate himself."

"He wouldn't be incriminating himself if he didn't kill the victim." Beau turns back to me. "You could spend a long time in prison if you get convicted of this crime. We can help you out."

"You can help out by moving on to the next question, Detective," Kieran returns.

Jocelyn interrupts. "Have you ever used any illegal drug, Mr. Espinosa? Or any drug at all that wasn't directly prescribed by a doctor?"

"How is that relevant to this investigation?" Kieran asks.

"Did Montgomery Sinclair use drugs?" she asks. "That you know of?"

"The victim's use or non-use of drugs isn't my client's concern, Detective," Kieran replies.

"The victim was found with traces of cocaine on his jacket," Beau tells us. "Does that ring a bell?"

I jolt out of my seat. "What?! That's impossible!"

Kieran lays his hand on my arm and surprises me. I spin around to stare at him and see him shooting me a warning look. I'm not supposed to talk to the Police—about any of this.

Montgomery couldn't have been using drugs. I will never believe that.

"The crime lab reports suggest that Mr. Espinosa had cocaine on his fingers at the time of his arrest." Beau's eyes dart to me. "Just tell the truth and spare yourself a lengthy, pointless trial."

My mind spins. I couldn't have had cocaine on my fingers, unless.....

"If the victim had cocaine on his jacket, then my client could have gotten the cocaine on his fingers while he was doing CPR, couldn't he?" Kiera suggests. "It sounds like we're done here, Detectives."

"You don't have to do this, Mr. Espinosa," Beau repeats.

I couldn't say anything if I tried. I'm going crazy with this information.

Montgomery didn't do drugs and neither did I. I can't think of anyone else who ever enters the Halcyon building who does drugs and who could have gotten close enough to kill him.

Kieran stands up and shakes hands with the two detectives. So does Mose. I stand up, but I'm too stunned to shake hands or even see straight.

I become aware of Jocelyn studying me extra closely. What is she thinking? Does she think my continual protests make me look guilty? I wouldn't be surprised. Everything makes me look guilty. I don't even know what could possibly make me look innocent.

The two detectives leave, but my nightmare is only just beginning. Now how am I supposed to get out of this?

Mose and Kieran escort me outside. We get into their firm's limo and they drive me back to their practice where we meet in their conference room.

Kieran turns on me the minute I get through the door. "What's this crap about you having cocaine on your fingers?! I told you to tell me everything!"

"I never touched the stuff! I've never done cocaine in my life! The killer must have had it on his fingers and gotten it on Montgomery's jacket."

"Just tell me the truth if you killed him, Diego!" Kieran fires back. "I can't defend you if I don't know the truth."

"I DIDN'T KILL MONTGOMERY, KIERAN!!" I roar. "I would have told you if I did! I found him stabbed to death on his office floor and I tried to do CPR! What more can I tell you?"

"You better not be lying to me! Now tell me where and how they found this cocaine on you.

"I don't know!! You were the one who said I could have gotten it on my hands when I was doing CPR! I didn't see anything on his jacket! He was covered in blood! *I* was covered in blood! I don't see how they could have found anything on my hands because I was dripping blood all over the place by the time the Police got there!"

"Well, it got there one way or the other, didn't it?"

I open my mouth to say something when his receptionist knocks on the door. She sticks her head in without waiting for us to answer. "Mr. Speight? There's a Detective Hitchcock from the NYPD here asking to see you—and Mr. Espinosa."

"What the hell does she want?" Kieran snarls. "We just left a meeting with her."

"She won't say, Sir. She says it's urgent."

He snorts. The receptionist is still standing there waiting for him to give his answer when Jocelyn shoves into the room. She actually makes the receptionist stumble against the door frame.

"Oh, thank God you're here, Diego!" she blurts out.

Kieran holds out his hand. "We already made ourselves available for questioning, Detective...."

"You don't understand! There never was any cocaine found on his fingers! Sergeant Kolter told us to doctor the reports to make it look like there was, but there wasn't. The department is going on a witch hunt to frame you, Mr. Espinosa. I don't know why except that you're in The Billionaires' Club and this is a high-profile case with a high-profile suspect. Sergeant Kolter basically already told us to come up with the evidence to frame you no matter what. He was the one who told us to tell you that we found cocaine on your hands and now he's drawing up a false toxicology report to say the crime lab found it, too."

"That is a very serious accusation, Detective," Kieran tells her.

She looks straight up into my eyes. "I didn't become a cop to frame innocent people for crimes they didn't commit. I'm telling you the truth. The department never should have arrested you considering how strong your alibi is. They only did it because you're a billionaire—and now they're doing this."

"Are you willing to report this to the Civil Complaint Review Board?" Kieran asks. "It doesn't do any good to tell us if you won't tell anyone else."

"I was already planning to—and I was also planning on talking to Beau about it. He got the same order from Sergeant Kolter and I know Beau is a stand-up guy. I just wanted to tell you first. We just found out this morning and the Sergeant showed us the phony toxicology report as soon as you left the station. I left work to come straight here."

"I think you better report this," Kieran tells her. "We'll discuss how to use this information in Diego's defense."

She turns back to me. "I'm sorry I suspected you—and I'm sorry I made your life uncomfortable these last few days. None of this ever should have happened. I got the wrong idea about you being in the club—and I guess the city did, too."

I'm too stunned to say anything to her. What *could* I say to her? I can't exactly thank her for being involved in framing me and potentially ruining my life."

She looks back and forth between me and Kieran before she walks out of the room.

"That was an interesting turn of events," Mose remarks.

"We'll meet again to strategize on how we can use this the right way," Kieran decides. "We can get the case dismissed, but she has to report it first. We'll be right back to square one if she doesn't."

Chapter 9: Diego

I have to take a few minutes to collect my wits before I get into the limo to go to the Halcyon building for the day. Heaven only knows what I'll find when I get there.

Whatever I find, for good or bad, I'll be handling it alone. I can't keep calling on my friends in The Billionaires' Club to come and bail me out. This business needs to sink or swim without Montgomery.

I always liked doing business with him. Now I remember why. I didn't like handling everything alone. I could always count on one other person to care enough to help me run the company.

I fall into deep thoughts on the way to the office. I need to bring someone else on as my new partner. I work better when I work with someone else. I don't trust anyone on the executive board to be that person.

I could promote Emerson. I know him. I like him and I trust him. He'll already be in line to inherit his father's shares in the company. That gives Emerson as much decision-making power as I have.

He's the logical choice—and he already knows as much as Montgomery ever did. Emerson is just as involved in all of Montgomery's business dealings.

I make up my mind to have a meeting with him later this week. I don't want to do it now. Emerson is still too broken up about his father's death. I don't want to load the guy with more than he can handle when he's already fragile.

He might not want to take over for Montgomery. Emerson might be reconsidering his direction in life. He might decide that losing his father has taken all the joy out of the process and he wants to do something else instead. I have to be ready for that.

I show up to work and walk in to find the place a few degrees less chaotic than it has been lately. We get the word from the Police Department that they're removing the cordon on the executive floor.

We can finally start bringing in professional cleaners to remove the carpet, repaint Montgomery's office, clean up all the blood stains, and get the floor ready for us to move back in.

The news relaxes everyone and the company starts to function more smoothly. Maybe that was the problem. Everyone was still jumpy after Montgomery's death. Now we can all put it behind us and move on—everyone except me, of course.

I have enough to do just keeping the business going. The Irish Ranger Wing finally got their shipment and they're satisfied with it. A few other confirmations come in during the day that we've completed delivery on our contracts and we're receiving payment.

I head off to the spare office I've been using this week, but I decide to stop by the bathroom on the way.

I walk in and hear sniffing. I stop dead in my tracks when I see Emerson standing in one of the stalls. He must have just ducked in here because he leaves the stall door open. I see exactly what he's doing.

He stands with his back to the room, bends over, and sniffs loudly at something in his hands. He does it five or six times, sniffs a few more times, and then rubs his nose before he turns around.

I stand rooted to the spot. He's holding a tiny baggie of white powder in one hand and a three-inch glass tube in the other.

His eyes fall out of their sockets when he sees me watching him. "Diego...." he stammers. "This isn't what it looks like....."

I don't stick around to hear anything else. I spin on my heels, storm out of the bathroom, and keep on going to leave the building. I didn't just see that. I didn't just see Emerson using cocaine in the company bathroom.

How long has he been using it? He must be really addicted if he's doing it at work. He could have been doing it for years. Did Montgomery know? I can't believe I actually considered making Emerson my business partner.

I keep walking down the street. I need to get as far away from this information as possible. What am I supposed to do about this?

Then I remember. Montgomery had cocaine on his jacket—and I know for an absolute fact that he never used the stuff. He absolutely hated drugs.

He despised anyone who used them. He thought only lowlifes and scumbags used drugs. He never would have done business with anyone who used drugs. He wouldn't have cared if the person was his own son.

The killer must have had cocaine on their hands when they killed him. Is Emerson the killer?

I rush off to Kieran's office to tell him what I found out. I can't take a car. I'm too wound up with too many conflicting ideas in my head.

How am I supposed to deal with Emerson now? How am I supposed to get him out of my company when he stands to inherit a controlling share of it?

I burst into the law firm and accost the receptionist. "I need to see Kieran right away! It's an emergency!"

"I'm sorry, Sir," she tells me. "He's out of the office at the moment. He's taking a personal day with his family. He's uncontactable. I can leave him a message if you want me to."

I grab my phone and call Kieran instead, but he doesn't pick up. Damn it.

I race outside. I have to do something about this—but what?

I'm just about to go back in and see about talking to Mose or Garrett. One of them will be able to tell me what to do.

I raise my head and get ready to go back inside when I spot Jocelyn across the street. She's putting money in her parking meter.

I charge across the street and almost collide with her. I skid to a halt all out of breath. "Emerson!" I gasp. "Emerson....Sinclair....."

She frowns at me. "What about him?"

"He.....he's the one......I just found him.....in the bathroom.....at work.....He was....he was snorting cocaine!"

Her eyebrows fly up. "Really? Wow."

"He was....the last one....who saw Montgomery....after I left...."

She nods. "Yeah, I got that. Just hold on a second. Let me check a few things."

She pulls out her phone, taps on it, and holds it to her ear. "Yeah, hey. Are you at your desk right now? I need you to look something up for me. Look up Emerson Sinclair. See if he has any record of using drugs." She moves the phone away from her mouth while we wait. "Beau is checking for us."

The seconds drag past. I feel myself shaking with nervous energy. It's happening. We're going to find out who really killed Montgomery. I sure as hell didn't do it.

I don't see Jocelyn as the enemy anymore. She knows I'm innocent. She's an ally. She's on my side trying to clear my name.

She finally talks into the phone again. "Great. Thanks a million. I'll see you in a little while." She hangs up. "Well, it's true. He has convictions for using, purchasing, and selling cocaine. It looks like we found our suspect."

I burst out in relieved laughter. I can't stop myself from beaming at her. I start to say, "Thank you, Detective!" before I realize what I'm doing.

I shouldn't be talking to her, smiling at her, or acting friendly with her. She's still working for the other side. I nod, thank her, and walk off in the other direction to get away from her. I shouldn't have talked to her in the first place.

I race away, and by the time I get back to the office, I hear from the other execs that Emerson has gone home for the day. They make it sound like he's too upset to work because he's still grief-stricken over his father's death.

I'd say he's more likely grief-stricken over getting caught.

Chapter 10: Jocelyn

"**I** sure hope you know what you're doing," Beau murmurs to me under his breath.

"I sure knew what I was doing when I became a cop," I tell him. "I did it to uphold the law, not to make certain people look bad and send them to prison just because certain other people wanted to make them look bad and send them to prison. Are you really going to stand there and keep your mouth shut while the department concocts the evidence to send an innocent man to prison?"

"No, but....Jesus, girl! You're taking on the NYPD! Do you know what this means?"

"Did the NYPD just wake up and become a criminal organization while I was asleep last night? I didn't sign up for this. One of us has to go. If the city doesn't play ball and drop the charges against Diego, then I'm outta here. This isn't the brand of justice I serve and neither should you."

He looks away. He won't stop squirming while we wait to go into Sergeant Kolter's office. Three men in suits from the Civil Complaints Review Board are already in there with the mayor and Chief of Police Jeremy Rodecker. It looks like my report got to the right people.

I hold a stack of file folders in my arm. Beau and I have been waiting a long time for all of them to call us inside.

I'm not going to lie. I'm shitting a brick about going in there, but it has to be done, especially after what we found out about Emerson.

He doesn't have an alibi for the time of his father's death. Emerson says he went home after the meeting between Montgomery, Diego, Kevin, and Paige. Emerson has no explanation for why he went home in the middle of the workday.

He was supposed to be shadowing his father around so Emerson could learn the business and eventually take over. Montgomery stayed at work, so Emerson should have been there—and maybe he was.

We haven't gotten around to asking the other executives if any of them saw Emerson go into his father's office right before the killing. We already know Diego wasn't in the building. We have enough to at least drop the charges against him.

The Chief Rodecker finally opens the door and calls me and Beau inside. Sergeant Kolter sits behind his desk glaring at everyone. He especially glares at me.

That's okay. I've gotten used to him glaring at me over the years. I consider it a privilege and a compliment that he's glaring at me now. It proves my point.

"Thank you for bringing this matter to our attention, Detective," the Complaints Commissioner tells me. His name is Ken Putnam. He's a tall, skinny guy with glasses. "We've gone over the contents of your report with Sergeant Kolter. Would you please reiterate this accusation for us so we can get to the bottom of this?"

I take a deep breath and lay my stack of folders on the desk in front of everyone. "Diego Espinosa has an ironclad alibi for the time of Montgomery Sinclair's death. Diego had no known motive, no criminal history, and performed CPR on the victim from the time he found the deceased until emergency services arrived. The department had no reasonable grounds to arrest this man or to hold him in custody or to question him about this killing. I don't believe the city ever would have done so if Diego Espinosa hadn't been a member of The Billionaires' Club. I believe Sergeant Kolter or whoever has been directing this investigation singled him out for that reason alone."

No one answers me. No one contradicts me, either, so maybe a few people in this room already know it's true.

"Sergeant Kolter gave me a direct order to find the evidence to pin this murder on Mr. Espinosa whether he was guilty or not. Sergeant Kolter ordered both Detective Herstead and me to fabricate evidence to make it look like Mr. Espinosa had cocaine on his hands at the time of his arrest when he didn't. Sergeant Kolter showed both of us a copy of a fake forensics report showing the existence of this cocaine when there wasn't any. I informed the suspect and his lawyer and then filed my report with the Review board. I have been protesting Mr. Espinosa's innocence since this case started and Sergeant Kolter turned a blind eye to the evidence. Mr. Espinosa informed me last week that he had caught Emerson Sinclair using cocaine in the company bathroom. Detective Herstead and I followed this up and found that the victim's son has a criminal history of drug use and trafficking. He has no alibi for the time of the murder, but Sergeant Kolter continues to ignore this line of inquiry to pursue his case against Mr. Espinosa."

Commissioner Putnam turns to Beau. "Can you confirm this report, Detective?"

Beau looks away in the other direction. "Yes, Sir. It's all true."

"Why didn't you support your partner's report then?" Police Chief Rodecker asks. "You let her report this alone. You didn't even sign the report."

Beau shrugs at nothing. "I guess I should have, Sir. I guess I just didn't want to get fired over it. I have a family to support."

"What do you have to say about this, Sergeant?" Commissioner Putnam takes a piece of paper out of the folio in his hands. "I have the crime lab report here detailing the presence of cocaine on Mr. Espinosa's fingers. This report was signed by Lance Hooper, the same lab technician who discovered the cocaine on the victim's jacket. He claims he never signed this report and that he never tested the blood on Mr. Espinosa's fingers, therefore the crime lab couldn't have issued this report. There are also certain marks on the report suggesting that an image of Mr. Hooper's signature was electronically copied and pasted there. Do you have anything to say about that?"

Sergeant Kolter grunts under his breath and casts a general glare around the room. "You'll never make this stick. You can't prove anything."

"Actually, Sergeant," Commissioner Putnam replies. "The Civil Complaints Review Board has jurisdiction over the Police Department, all its personnel contracts, all criminal investigations, and individual use of department property. You're fired. I'll give you half an hour to leave the building."

Sergeant Kolter's eyes snap to Commissioner Putnam's face. "You can't do that!"

Commissioner Putnam pulls out his phone. "Do I need to call the Police to drag you out of the building?"

Sergeant Kolter opens his mouth to say something, shuts it, hesitates for a second, and then stands up and walks out of the room. Commissioner Putnam sighs and passes his hand across his eyes.

"I'm ordering all of you to drop the charges against Diego Espinosa," he announces. "Continue pursuing your case against the victim's son, Detective."

"Yes, Sir," I tell him. "Thank you."

"Thank you, Detective. I wish the whole Force was like you."

He walks out followed by the mayor, Chief Rodecker, and the other two Review Board members. They leave me and Beau standing in the empty sergeant's office.

Beau lets out a shaky sigh of relief. "You dodged a bullet on that one, girl."

"I didn't dodge anything. You're the one who dodged a bullet. They could have charged you for obstruction of justice. You should know better, Beau."

He casts a glance toward Sergeant Kolter's desk. "I wonder who they'll get to replace him."

"That's their business. Let's get out of here. We have work to do."

Chapter 11: Diego

I drag my ass into The Billionaires' Club. I try to pretend I'm okay and getting through the day, but I'm not. This whole murder case drags me down.

I greet a few people and share a few meaningless snatches of conversation before the club meeting starts. The officers present their agenda, talk about a few upcoming events, and other business that doesn't concern me.

I haven't been able to go back to the Halcyon building since I caught Emerson using cocaine in the bathroom. I don't know if Jocelyn has filed her report yet or if she reported it. I don't know how long it takes for these things to happen. She might not have done anything.

I shouldn't expect her to. I shouldn't expect anything other than for this case to go to trial.

I sense the rest of the club members tiptoeing around me, especially the ones who talked to Jocelyn during her visit to the club.

The meeting breaks up without it touching on me at all. It isn't like planning our next gala can get me out of a murder charge.

I wander around going through the motions of talking to people. I eventually end up in a group with Kevin, Paige, and the other officers. They're talking about Kevin setting up People, Inc. branches in other countries.

"I want to talk to you about this whole Russian army contract deal you mentioned," he tells me. "I've been talking to the Russian version of the State Department. They're gung-ho about me doing this training on Russian soil—which means we would need to go ahead with the contract before we can set up and get the project up and running."

I nod. "We can do that. When do you want to talk about it?"

"Can't we talk about it now? That's what I meant. I want to talk to you about it now."

"Oh! I understand now. I'm sorry."

He starts to smile at me, but my phone rings just then. It's Kieran, so I answer it. "Hello?"

"They dropped the charges, pal!" he yells into the phone. "You're clear. Your guardian angel Hitchcock came through for you after all. The case is dropped and Sergeant Kolter just got terminated from the Police Department. I just got the call from her a few minutes ago. The detectives have been ordered to pursue the case against Emerson. You're free, man! You're all done. It's over!"

I turn away from the group so they don't see me getting emotional. I sense Kevin standing behind me listening to this, and like magic, his hand appears on my shoulder and squeezes.

I choke on the words. "Thank you, Kieran."

"It wasn't me, man. That detective pulled your ass out of the fire. You should really take her to dinner or something. She put her neck on the line for you and it paid off. She could have lost everything bringing an accusation like that. She's the one you should be thanking."

I nod at nothing. I can barely make myself heard. "Okay. Thank you. I better go."

I hang up and stare at my phone. It's over. I can't even turn around to face my friends. Tears spring to my eyes. I'm free.

The silence behind me tells a different story. Kevin must have heard Kieran yelling into the phone. I turn around to find the whole group watching me. They know. Kevin must have told them.

"Congratulations, man," Judah murmurs. "We never stopped believing in you."

I compress my lips and nod as they all surround me, hug me, and pat me on the back. I wipe tears of relief off my cheeks. I can't stop shaking. I can't believe it's really over.

"We should go out to celebrate or something," Lane suggests. "Come on, Diego. Let us take you out to dinner. You've had a hell of a month."

I try to make myself stop nodding. "Thank you all, my friends. You don't know how grateful I am for your support. I should be taking you out to dinner."

Those words bring back Kieran's words. Jocelyn is the one I should be taking out to dinner. She's the one who gave me this. She saved my life—literally.

She's the best cop I've ever met. She risked it all to do what was right. I'm standing here getting congratulated right now because of her. Not even Kieran supported me the way she did.

My friends take me out to dinner and we all sit around laughing, joking, talking, and enjoying ourselves, but I can't get her out of my mind. She's a genuinely good person. She believes in justice and she believes in the law. I can only respect that.

She did her job. I didn't think she would. I thought she would be one of those people who tried to nail me to the wall just because.

Kevin bumps my shoulder to get my attention at the dinner table. "So what do you think about the Russia deal?"

"I'll contact my people to get in touch with your people. We'll get the contract underway....and I suppose you'll need to arrange things with your lovely wife to send you some of her equipment to train the Russian personnel."

"I can do that." He touches his glass to mine. "I'm on friendly terms with the company CEO."

I laugh. "I certainly hope so. Now I want to talk to you about something, Kevin—something of a personnel matter I'm dealing with."

He spreads his hands. "Lay it on me. I'm your man."

"It's about Emerson. I want to get rid of him, but I obviously can't. He owns too big a stake in the company."

"Not if he gets convicted of murdering his father, he doesn't."

"He hasn't gotten convicted yet and I can't remove him until he does get convicted."

"Then your only option is to suspend him."

"How can I do that when he's innocent until proven guilty? I wouldn't want someone to suspend me just because the Police Department decided to accuse me of murder. Emerson might be innocent—as innocent as I am. Some other coke addict could have killed Montgomery."

Kevin makes a face at me. "Will you listen to yourself? What other coke addict had access to Montgomery's office and could get inside without raising anyone's suspicions?"

"That isn't the point, my friend. I need to bring in certain key people to take up the slack. I don't have to remove him outright—not until he gets convicted. I just want to relieve him of as much responsibility as possible—which means I need people. These would be C-suite level people—the best. I don't know who else to turn to besides you. Can you help me out?"

He stares into his glass. "That's going to be a tough one, but not impossible."

"And I don't want to keep relying on you and the other club members. You've already done enough and you all have your own businesses to run."

"You know we have no problem helping out," he counters. "We want to."

"I'm certain that you do and I'm also certain you wouldn't want to do it on an ongoing, long-term, or permanent basis."

He shrugs and looks down into his glass. "Okay. You're right."

"So I need people, Kevin. I need good people."

"I'll see what I can do, but it might take time."

"I understand. I'm willing to wait for the right people. I only want the best. I don't want someone I have to get rid of later. If you can't find them, no one can."

He smiles at me. "How are you going to deal with Emerson after this?"

"God only knows," I groan. "I dread even facing him."

"Maybe he'll make himself scarce, now that you know his secret."

"I can only hope. I hope the Police Department concludes their case quickly. I can't live with this strain."

Chapter 12:
Jocelyn

I pace up and down in front of the closed courtroom doors. "Will you settle down?" Beau snaps at me. "You're driving me nuts."

"I can't keep still," I mutter. "I'm really nervous."

"Well, I would be fine if you weren't making me nervous. Just go sit down over there."

He points to some benches along the wall. We have the courtroom lobby to ourselves. I go over to the bench, but the courtroom doors open before I get there. Beau and I both jump out of our skin when one of the bailiffs calls us in.

Beau sits in the gallery while I go up to the witness box. Diego is already there. He must already have testified against Emerson.

The court clerk swears me in and I take the stand. District Attorney Jillian McAfee stands up to question me. "Would you please describe for the court how you came to pursue your investigation against Emerson Sinclair?"

"The Police Department originally pursued a case against Diego Espinosa in the death of Montgomery Sinclair, the accused's father. The crime lab discovered evidence of cocaine residue on the victim's jacket, but he had no trace of the substance in his bloodstream. The location and position of the traces indicated that the victim engaged in a struggle with the murderer before the killer stabbed Mr. Sinclair."

"Your initial investigation led you to believe that Mr. Espinosa left these traces on the victim's jacket. Isn't that correct?"

"No, Ma'am. My investigation never indicated anything of the kind. Mr. Espinosa's hands were covered in blood at the time of the victim's death. We couldn't have discovered traces on him even if they had been there. The suggestion that Mr. Espinosa had cocaine on his hands was never substantiated. Even if the cocaine had been there, he could have picked up the traces while he was doing CPR on the victim. There was never any evidence that Mr. Espinosa or Montgomery Sinclair ever did drugs or had any contact with them."

"And you are the investigating detective who discovered that Emerson Sinclair did have a history of drug use. Isn't that correct?"

"Actually, Mr. Espinosa was the one who discovered Emerson Sinclair's history and brought it to my attention. I don't think any of us considered Emerson a suspect before Mr. Espinosa found out that Emerson was a cocaine addict."

"Security camera footage from the Halcyon Commercial Holdings building suggests that Emerson Sinclair left the building the way he said he was going to, that he returned through a side entrance where he didn't think anyone would see him, and that he waited for the receptionist and the other executives to leave on their lunch break before returning to his father's office unseen."

"Yes, Ma'am. The footage shows him entering the building and crossing the executive floor. We don't have any footage of anything that happened inside Montgomery Sinclair's office because Emerson shut the door while he was in there."

"And the footage also includes him leaving the office, shutting the door behind him, and leaving the building by the same route."

"Yes, Ma'am. That's correct."

"Do you have any evidence that Mr. Espinosa returned to the building?"

"No, Ma'am, but we do have several hundred witness statements that he was across town at the time. He was giving a speech at a college scholarship awards ceremony. He didn't return to the building. He couldn't have returned to the building."

"Thank you, Detective," DA McAfee sits down.

Emerson has hired Mustafa Edwards as his lawyer. Mustafa is a killer. I'm going to have to be careful in my answers to him.

"Do you have any personal connection with Mr. Espinosa, Detective?" Mustafa asks.

I jolt and spin around. "What? Of course not!"

"In what context did he tell you that my client used cocaine?"

"I was parking my car and Mr. Espinosa came up to me on the street. He was all out of breath and he told me that he had just caught Emerson Sinclair using cocaine in the bathroom of their office building."

"Are you sure you didn't meet Mr. Espinosa privately at which time he cast suspicion on his dead partner's son to take the heat off himself?"

"I never met Mr. Espinosa privately in any context ever. I've never even been alone in a room with him before or after the murder."

"Why do you think he approached you in such an informal context without his attorney present if it wasn't personal?"

"He approached me right outside his attorney's office. I assumed he had just come from there and couldn't get in touch with his attorney right then. Mr. Espinosa was extremely agitated about making this discovery. I got the impression that he needed to tell someone right away. It was his information that led me to check Emerson Sinclair's criminal record to find out if there was anything to it."

"Was there ever anything of a personal nature in your dealings with Mr. Espinosa during the course of this investigation?"

"Quite the contrary," I reply. "He was extremely hostile at first."

"What made him change to become less hostile?"

"I don't know what changed it on his side except that I told him and his attorney about the Police Department's efforts to convict him of a crime for which he never should have gotten arrested. I apologized to him for my part in that even though I had been trying to clear his name since the beginning. In my opinion, Mr. Espinosa never was a suspect of this crime. He was never a suspect in any crime except that of being much richer than the rest of us—which I suppose some people consider a crime."

"No further questions, Your Honor." Mustafa sits down. "The defense rests."

"You're excused, Detective," the judge tells me.

I go out to the gallery and sit down next to Beau. I make one brief moment of eye contact with Diego before the judge gets everyone's attention.

"The court finds that the indictment of murder in the first degree against Emerson Sinclair is sustained," the judge announces. "The suspect will be remanded in custody to the New York State penal system for trial and held without bail. Court is dismissed."

The judge strikes his gavel and the courtroom breaks up. The bailiffs cuff Emerson and lead him away. DA McAfee shakes hands with Mustafa and they talk at the front of the courtroom for a minute.

Beau and I also stand up. Diego meets us in the aisle on our way out of the courtroom. He extends his hand to me. "Thank you, Detective. I can never thank you enough. I am forever in your debt."

"I was just doing my job. I'm glad it worked out for you. You deserve it. I hope you'll continue to do all your good works in the world. We need more people like you."

He blushes and his dark eyes twinkle. He takes extra long letting go of my hand. "You are too kind to say so. It never hurts to have good people like you who are willing to go the distance for what is right. I won't forget this. I wish you all the best in the world."

He leaves me and Beau alone. "Who would have thought a billionaire could be a decent guy?" Beau asks me.

"Something tells me a lot more of them are like this than most people think."

Chapter 13: Diego

I stride into The Billionaires' Club and look around the room. Everyone is already here. I see Kevin at a distance, but he's already talking to three people. Everyone wants to talk to Kevin, so I don't go near him yet.

I go to the buffet instead. I haven't eaten lunch. I've been saving my appetite for this.

I'm helping myself to the crab salad when Rory comes up to me. He startles me by clapping me on the shoulder from behind. "Just the man I was hoping to see," he tells me.

"Why do you want to see me?" I ask. "You're the PR guy here. I should be coming to see you to salvage my reputation."

He laughs. "There's nothing wrong with your reputation. I, on the other hand....." He trails off.

"I'm sure your reputation is as spotless as you could wish. What do you want to talk to me about?"

"Your new PR exec contacted me on Wednesday. He said he was looking for a firm to manage Halcyon's image. He said he doesn't want the company to become known as an international arms broker."

I frown at him. "How bizarre. We don't deal in arms."

"I asked him if he had talked to you about this and he said no. That's when I decided to tell you myself."

I groan and turn back to the crab salad. "Wonderful," I mutter. "I told him last week I wanted him to take more initiative. This isn't what I had in mind."

"I told him we would be happy to take on Halcyon as a client as long as he got the whole executive team on board."

I snort at him. "You are so clever, Rory. I really need to take lessons from you."

He grins at me. "I'm sure you can take it from here, big guy."

"Oh, I will. Don't worry." I frown at him. "How are you? I never see you anymore."

He opens his mouth to answer when Kevin comes over to us. "Just the man I was hoping to find," he tells me and then turns to Rory. "I want to talk to you, too, when you have a minute."

"I have a minute and we're talking. What's on your mind?"

"I'm opening two more overseas branches, a second one in Russia and a second one in China. I want you to handle PR for the roll-out." Kevin turns back to me. "Are we ready to go with the contract negotiations?"

"We're ready and our Russian counterparts are in town staying at the Hyatt Grand Central. They're very excited to meet you—but I think we should take them out to dinner tonight to break the ice—you, me, and Paige. I don't want tomorrow's negotiation to be the first time they meet us. I want us to become friends first."

"Okay, good idea. Let me call Paige." He pulls out his phone. I catch Rory watching us.

"How's it going for you, man?" he asks while we wait.

"It's going excellently for me. Thank you for asking. The new executives are working out very well. I'm happy with how the company is growing—apart from this latest fluke, I mean."

He laughs. "I'm sure you'll work it out. How do you feel after six months of running the company alone since you lost Montgomery and bought out Emerson?"

"I didn't exactly buy him out. The court confiscated his shares as part of his plea deal. The court put them on the open market and I bought them. I made sure to buy them. I was standing on the sidelines with the bills crumpled in my sweaty hand waiting to buy them to make sure no one else got to them first."

"That sounds like you're happy running the company alone."

"I don't want to get into this mess again. I don't want to go through the same tornado if something happens to my next business partner and I'm left to pick up the pieces. I would rather just hold the pieces now and handle them all along. Then I don't have to wonder if my partner is forgetting something critical or if I'll find him murdered on the floor of his office one day."

"I guess we'll never know why Emerson did it," he remarks.

"I don't care why he did it. I never want to go through that again."

Kevin gets off the phone just then. "Paige is on her way down. She'll meet us here and then the three of us can go pick up the Russians."

I laugh. "You have to stop calling them that, my friend."

"Why? They *are* Russian." Kevin turns to Rory. "Do you want to come with us? We're going out to dinner. You're more than welcome."

"I don't know if I should," he replies. "I don't want to intrude if you're going to be discussing your contract."

"We won't be discussing anything formally," I tell him. "This is just dinner. We won't do any serious negotiating until tomorrow."

He shrugs. "All right. I'll come."

Kevin pats him on the back. "Excellent. Then you and I can talk international relations."

The three of us take our leave of the other club members. It's already getting late by the time we go outside. A limo pulls up to the curb. We get in to find Paige Novak waiting there for us.

She greets Rory and hugs him. "My favorite PR guy," she exclaims.

"What about me?" Kevin asks.

She laughs at him. "I like you for other things."

He kisses her and puts his arm around her on the seat. We chat about our mutual business deals on our way to the Hyatt Grand Central.

We enter the lobby where we meet three Russian military officers waiting for us. They're all colonels, but they come in suits for dinner. I hope they come in suits for tomorrow's negotiation, but they probably won't.

I introduce everyone and explain that Rory is just a friend in The Billionaires' Club and he's only coming for social reasons, not to take part in the negotiation.

He starts speaking Russian to the generals and they all explode into rapid talk. Then Kevin surprises the pants off of all of us by speaking Russian to the generals, too. Even his wife stares at him with her mouth open.

Paige and I exchange glances. This is not how I expected tonight to go. Rory and Kevin talk fast and make the generals laugh. I clear my throat with difficulty and suggest that we all go out to dinner.

We get back into Paige's and Kevin's limo. It takes us to a fancy Italian restaurant downtown. We sit in the booth where everyone talks to everyone else. The generals speak English and one of them even speaks Spanish.

I talk to him in Spanish for a while. Then they talk to Paige in English and Kevin joins in while I talk to Rory about his work. He runs a mega-international PR firm handling the images of politicians, celebrities, organizations, and even whole countries.

Conversation fires back and forth. I don't know what Rory and Kevin are talking to the generals about in Russian. I don't hear anyone talking about tomorrow's negotiation.

I turn aside from the table to flag the waiter to bring us some appetizers. That's when I see Jocelyn Hitchcock across the restaurant from our table.

She's wearing her usual leather jacket and looks as timeless as ever. She makes eye contact with me and stands up from a table where she's sitting across from one guy. He's a white guy about her age.

He sits with his back to me. I can't tell if she's on a date with him or not.

She smiles at me for a split second before she walks off to the bar. She doesn't approach me just as I don't approach her.

She certainly looks like she's been doing well these last six months since the investigation wrapped. She really is beautiful in a classic, everyday way.

I don't know why she fascinates me so much. It isn't like she's the most glamorous woman on the planet. I should know. I've seen plenty of glamorous women in my time.

I should go back to my conversation with my friends and the Russians, but just as I'm about to turn my head, two other guys in business casual come up to her at the bar. They're twice her size and they know it.

They flank her on either side while she's talking to the bartender. The two dudes stand way too close, and when she tries to back away, they box her in even tighter. She looks back and forth between them. I would have to be blind not to see her gearing up to defend herself.

The guy she left sitting at the table doesn't notice anything. He has his face glued to his phone. I don't know who this joker is, but he doesn't deserve the time in her day if he doesn't at least stand up to protect her when she needs him to.

She's a cop, so I'm sure she knows a few things about how to take care of herself, but I can't just sit here and leave her on her own.

I stand up without a word of explanation to my table companions, cross the room, and shove myself between her and the dude on the left. I straight-arm the other guy to push him away.

"Back off, fellas," I tell them. "Leave the lady alone."

"Who the hell are you—her boyfriend?" the dude on her other side demands.

"It doesn't matter who I am. I don't think she invited you to get in her face. Now back off before you wind up getting hauled downtown in handcuffs."

"What are *you* gonna do about it?" the guy behind me snaps. "There's only one of you and two of us."

I don't tell the moron that she would be the one to haul them downtown in handcuffs. They don't need to know that. I also don't tell them that there are two of us. There is no doubt in my mind that she's the better fighter.

I put my arm behind her back, steer her away from the bar, and back toward the table where she was sitting before. The guy she was talking to is long gone. What an asshole. He saw her in trouble and bounced right out on her.

"Are you okay?" I ask her.

She nods up at me with those big, wide, bottomless eyes. God, she's so beautiful! "That was really sweet of you," she murmurs. "Thank you."

"Please tell me you weren't on a date with that guy and he ran away when he saw you in danger."

"I wasn't on a date with him. He's an informant on one of our investigations. He probably didn't want anyone to notice him meeting me. That's why he left."

"Are you going to be okay? Let me give you a ride home."

She smiles at me. "You're a prince, Diego."

"Come on. Let's get out of here." I steer her toward the door and cast one glance up toward the table where Rory, Kevin, and Paige sit talking to the Russians. Kevin and Rory both see me and Kevin raises his hand to wave at me as I lead Jocelyn out of the restaurant.

I call my limo driver and he comes to pick me up. I open the door to let her into the car and then climb in after her.

"Thank you again for your help tonight," she murmurs in the darkness. Streetlights sweep past the windows and light up her features every few seconds. "I really wasn't looking forward to dealing with those two."

"How have you been since the investigation ended?" I ask.

"That was only one of many. All the others are still ongoing. It never ends."

"You look good. You look like life is treating you well."

She smiles at me. "I can't complain. You look good, too. You look a lot better than you did during the investigation."

I snort. "I don't think it will ever get as bad as that. I can take comfort in that. The worst is over for me."

She bursts into a full grin. "I'll remember never to get accused of murder."

I get her address and give it to the driver. "I hope your informant doesn't mind you telling me about him," I tell her. "You can assure him that I never saw his face."

"I will tell him that. I'm sure he'll be relieved."

"I thought you were on a date with him. I thought he must be a loser for leaving you in trouble like that."

She giggles. "I don't date, Diego. Are you kidding? No one wants to date an NYPD homicide detective."

I frown at her. "Why not?"

"They think it's like the movies. They think it's running around getting into gun battles against mobsters and stuff like that. They don't know being a detective is really a desk job more than anything. I've had a few dates scream and run when I told them what I do for a living."

"They didn't really, literally scream and run, did they? They didn't throw up their hands in horror, scream, and go running from the building."

She laughs. "Maybe not as bad as that, but I have had three different guys get up from the table in the middle of the conversation and walk straight out of the building in the middle of the date."

I gape at her with my mouth open. "Are you serious?"

She nods and her eyes twinkle. "Yep."

"What absolute trolls. I would never do that."

She laughs. "I'm sure every woman wants to date you."

I pretend she didn't just say that. "I *have* decided not to see someone again when I found out what they did for a living, but I at least ended the date, paid for it, and drove the person home afterward. Then I had to explain why I didn't want to see them again, but at least I was polite about it. That's the bare minimum as far as I'm concerned."

"Why did you decide not to see them again?"

"One of them was a hardcore sadistic dominatrix who wanted to keep her love slave chained to the kitchen door to service her when she got home from servicing all of her clients at work."

She bursts out in laughter. "Really?"

"Beating her slave was a necessary part of foreplay for her, so I had to tell her I didn't think we were compatible."

She won't stop laughing. "I'm relieved to hear that."

"Another one was a social justice warrior who thought everyone with a net worth over a hundred thousand dollars should have their assets confiscated and distributed to the poor. She thought all businesses should be run by the government and all big business CEOs and owners should be rounded up and held in concentration camps to protect the public from their poisonous influence."

She beams at me. "Aw. What a shame. Did she not know about you before you went out with her?"

"No, she didn't. I met her at a charity function. I'm not sure why she was there if she didn't know I was on the charity's Board of Trustees. We got talking and exchanged numbers and went out on a date. What we did for a living somehow never came up until then. We had too many other things to talk about, but it came out in the end."

I glance out the window as the limo pulls up in front of her apartment building. She smiles at me one more time. "Thank you for the ride—and thank you for your help tonight. It's nice to know there are a few real gentlemen still out there."

"Of course. Please don't hesitate to call on me if you need anything at all. I'm at your service." I get out and give her my hand to help her out. We face each other on the sidewalk.

We aren't even doing anything, but something compels me toward her. I want to kiss her right now, but that would be unprofessional. That's all we are to each other. We're acquaintances who once knew each other.

"Good night," I tell her. "I hope you have a good evening."

"You, too. I'm sure I'll see you around sometime." She goes to unlock the door of her building, smiles at me over her shoulder, and waves. "Bye."

I raise my hand to wave and she disappears inside. I get back in the limo and drive off. I text Kevin on the way. *What's happening there?*

The Russians are going to their hotel. They're jetlagged and they want to get some sleep before tomorrow's negotiation. Paige and I are going home and Rory already left. You might as well go home, too.

I will. You have a good evening.

How is Jocelyn? he asks.

She's fine. I just drove her home.

Good for you for stepping in and helping her, he tells me. *That was the right thing to do.*

My heart swells a little more. Of course he understands why I had to leave the table.

I text him, *I'll see you tomorrow. Sleep well.*

You, too. Good night.

I put my phone away and tell the driver to take me home. I need to catch up on sleep, too. Tomorrow is an important day and I want to be rested.

Chapter 14: Jocelyn

B eau and I roll into Sergeant Mayweather's office. He's been our sergeant for a year since Sergeant Kolter got fired.

Sergeant Mayweather is a much younger, bulldog-type of guy. He never laughs and he always looks furious, but he's the nicest guy in the world and he's the fairest boss I've ever worked for.

He would never fudge with the law—ever. That's the thing about him. He's more committed to the law than we are. He's downright inspiring that way. None of us ever has to question his integrity.

He's also as big and strong as an ox. He can take any man in the department in the boxing ring, on the wrestling mat, or on the shooting range. No one in the department can hold a candle to him.

He makes a habit of sitting out of our competitions because it's no contest with him. It wouldn't be fair for him to compete. It would be a one-horse race.

He waves a file folder at me and then at Beau. "I want you two to take over this one, " he snarls in his chesty, guttural voice. "It just came in last night. Caucasian male shot in the head on the corner of Broadway and 22nd Street. No prints found anywhere at the scene, of course, and no bullet found."

"How can the guy have been shot and no bullet found?" Beau asks.

"The shot was a clean through-and-through to the left eye socket. The bullet exited the back of the skull and hit a brick wall behind the victim. The killer must have taken both the bullet and the shell casing with him."

"That doesn't leave us a lot to go on, does it?" I point out.

"You got that right," Sergeant Mayweather snarls. "Forensic analysis suggests the killer came out of a subway station nearby, intercepted the victim as he was coming out of a neighboring building, walked up to him on the street corner and blammo! It was two-thirty in the morning—no witnesses—and no one in the surrounding buildings heard the gunshot—so the killer may have used a silencer."

"Wow. That sounds awfully premeditated," I add.

"It had to be. The victim was Romeano Pinkerton. He ran one of Clemente Barraco's money-laundering pool halls. Let's kick off the festivities by assuming the killing had something to do with Barraco's operation." He holds out the file folder for me to take. "Get out of here and go make your run for the end zone. I'll see you at the victory celebration."

Beau and I go back to our desks and start doing the preliminary keyboard work on all the usual cast of characters.

We already know chapter and verse on Clemente Barraco's operation including all the businesses in town that are really money-laundering fronts for his criminal organization.

We also know more than we ever wanted to know about Romeano Pinkerton. He was a professional scumbag and full-time asshole.

"I can name you fifty people right off the top of my head who would want to snuff Pinkerton," Beau mutters over his computer. "Including Barraco himself."

"Then let's start with them," I tell him. "Let's start playing Pin-the-Tail-On-the-Donkey and find out who had alibis for the time of the murder."

Beau looks up. "I bet you Pinkerton did business with people other than Barraco. I bet you we could find people who aren't part of Barraco's organization who also laundered money with Pinkerton. He didn't only work for Barraco, you know."

I stand up. "Come with me, my fine friend. I know where we can find out."

We leave the station and go to the Corner Pocket Pool Hall where Pinkerton did business. The place is in an uproar because Romeano isn't here to hold the place together anymore.

We ask to see his books. His accountant is more than happy to hand them over to us. None of these people wants to get busted for protecting Barraco.

"We don't have a prayer of touching Barraco anyway," Beau points out on our way back to the station. "His lawyers would run rings around us even if he *was* the one who popped Pinkerton."

We start going over Pinkerton's books and drawing up a list of names. The majority of Pinkerton's ledger entries are directly connected to Barraco's other front businesses. They all channel their ill-gotten loot through the pool hall.

"He converts all that cash into quarters, runs them through his pool tables a few hundred times, and then trades them in for bills," I point out. "It's a perfect system."

"Then how are we supposed to find out who killed Pinkerton?" Beau asks.

My heart stops and I point at a page in the ledger. "Right there, Beau. That's the answer right there."

He cranes his neck around to read the entry. "Spiderware. I don't recognize it. What is that—a game arcade or something?"

"No, genius. It's a tech company, of course. They write operating systems that run some of the most sophisticated equipment in the world. Think NASA, the biggest militaries, government espionage agencies—you name it. Even big-time operators like Boeing use Spiderware."

"Why would a company like that run its money through Pinkerton's pool tables?"

"They aren't. Someone is using that word as a code name."

"*Who* is using it, though? That's what I'm asking."

I tap on my computer and bring up one man's face. "Demetrius Runyon—Spiderware CEO. He was born and raised in the South Bronx—and he's a member of The Billionaires' Club. He's one of the few billionaire members who actually grew up in New York."

"What does that have to do with anything?"

"I don't know, but if Spiderware is showing up in Pinkerton's books, either the company or someone in it was laundering money through the Corner Pocket."

"What are we going to do about that? We can't just roll up and start bombarding these rich guys with questions. They'll lawyer up faster than anything."

That gives me an idea. "You start questioning Barraco's people. Find out who had alibis for the time of the murder."

"What good will that do us? None of these people will be the killer. If they're on Pinkerton's books, they would have hired someone on contract to whack Pinkerton. Why do you think the killer was so careful to cover his tracks?"

"Just go talk to them, okay? I think I know a way to talk to people in The Billionaires' Club without them lawyering up."

He rolls his eyes and groans. "Don't tell me what the way is, okay? I don't want to know."

"I wasn't planning to tell you anything. What do you think I am—stupid?"

We split up. I get on my phone, call Diego Espinosa, and ask him if he can get me into the club to talk to a few people about the investigation.

"Why do you want to talk to people in the club about an investigation?" he asks. "Is someone in the club a suspect?"

"I wouldn't call them a suspect—no."

"Then why do you want to talk to us? You wouldn't be coming to talk to us at all if someone in the club wasn't relevant to the investigation. Just tell me what it is and who it is. I won't be able to get you in if you don't tell me."

I take a deep breath. He's right—and I trust him with the information. "Okay, look. The victim is Romeano Pinkerton. He was a money-laundering agent for crime boss Clemente Barraco. We found a whole lot of people on Pinkerton's books who work for Barraco. We already know the victim was running Barraco's money through the business—but we found other people's names on the books, too—people who don't work for Barraco. One of the names is a company owned by a member of your club. That's the truth. I want to question him and the rest of you about his activities. We don't know if he's a suspect yet. We just want to get more information before we decide *who* to suspect."

His tone changes instantly. "Who is it?"

"I'm not sure if I should tell you."

"You better tell me," he snaps. "One of us could be doing business with this man and he could be running *our* money through some mobster's operation. This man could be implicating us without our knowledge. We have to know! Come on, Jocelyn! I know you wouldn't want any of us to get caught in a situation like that when we had no idea he was doing it. Would you want me to get caught in that situation? I can't believe that about you."

"No.....but...."

"Tell me who it is. I swear to you that, if you tell me who it is, I'll get you into the club. You have my word on that—but I have to know who it is."

I gulp. "It's Demetrius Runyon from Spiderware."

He goes dangerously quiet for a second. When he does speak, he growls in a deadly undertone. "Meet me outside the building in an hour. I'll get you in."

Chapter 15:
Jocelyn

I drive across town, park my car, and approach the security guards standing out in front of The Billionaires' Club. The same skinny white kid squints at me. "Can I help you, Ma'am?" he asks.

I flash him my badge. "I'm supposed to meet Diego Espinosa here at three o'clock."

He checks his watch, shrugs, and goes back to standing guard. Diego doesn't come out of the building until the stroke of three.

"I've told them all you're coming in and why," he tells me. "I've also told them not to give you any information that you might use to incriminate Demetrius."

"Is he here?"

"Yes, he's here, but he won't talk to you about the investigation without his lawyer present."

I nod. "I can't argue with that."

"You said you aren't even sure if he is a suspect, so you can ask any questions you want of the rest of us. You know the drill."

"Thank you."

He leads me inside. The scene is almost identical to the last meeting I attended except that there are a lot more women here today.

I recognize Paige Novak from the Montgomery Sinclair case. I also recognize Melody Gottlieb. They're both always in the press a lot because they're two of the very few female billionaires in the club.

Diego escorts me to one of the groups of people talking. I don't see anyone watching TV or working on computers this time. They all just stand around talking and pretending I'm not here.

I spot Demetrius Runyon right away. He's tall—about six-foot-three—with broad shoulders, light blonde hair, blue eyes, and hawkish features. He pretends not to see me even though Diego must have given him the same warning he gave the rest of them.

Diego stops next to Judah Hayes again. "Welcome back, Detective," Dante tells me. "I wish it could be under different circumstances."

"I wish that, too. I wish I didn't always have to come see you only when something goes wrong."

"So what's the story with this mob killing?" Giovanni asks. "What makes you think one of us had something to do with it?"

"We're investigating everyone with a business connection to the victim. He was involved in a money-laundering operation. Spiderware's name turned up on his books. We don't know if someone from the company was involved or if someone just used that as a code name. It could be either one."

"No one from Spiderware would be stupid enough to use that name," Jackson points out. "No one would deliberately leave a clue that would lead you back to the company. That would just be bone-headed."

I find myself smiling at him. "Criminals can do some pretty bone-headed things. Besides, right now, we don't have anything other than the name to link Spiderware to the criminal organization. That's why no one involved in the company is a suspect yet."

Demetrius Runyon comes over to us just then. Diego backs up to make room for Demetrius to join us. I do the same thing.

Demetrius levels me with a direct stare. "Detective. To what do I owe the pleasure?"

"I was just explaining to your associates here that the Spiderware name showed up on Romeano Pinkerton's money-laundering books. Romeano turned up dead last night, so we're following up with everyone who did business with him. We don't suspect you because literally anyone could have used that word as a code name. I just wanted to ask you about it."

"Don't tell her anything, Demetrius," Diego tells him.

"She says I'm not a suspect," Demetrius replies.

"You aren't," I tell him. "We have no reason to suspect you—unless you *were* laundering money through Pinkerton's books."

"What she means is that you aren't a suspect *yet*," Diego reminds him. "Don't tell her anything without your lawyer present."

I shoot him a look. Why is he interfering so much after I helped him in his own investigation?

"Can you tell me where you were last night?" I ask Demetrius.

He exchanges glances with Diego and Diego shakes his head. "I think I better not discuss this without my lawyer present." Demetrius pulls out his business card. "If you call that number, we can schedule a time to meet where you can question me *with* my lawyer present."

I ask a few more pointed questions of him and the other billionaires. It turns out that quite a few of them do business with Spiderware. Even Diego does business with Spiderware.

I'm not getting anywhere here, so I eventually give up and leave. Diego follows me outside.

I lose my patience on the sidewalk and turn on him once we get that far. "How could you do that to me?" I snap. "How could you humiliate me in front of all those people?"

"I wasn't trying to humiliate you, Jocelyn, but you can't expect me to let you incriminate a man who might be innocent. You said you don't even consider Demetrius a suspect at this point."

"You stonewalled me in front of everyone. You made me look like a fool in there, undermined my credibility, and blocked my investigation. You're free right now because of me. Do I have to remind you of that? I risked my entire career for you and this is how you repay me?"

"I'm very aware of that, Jocelyn, and I'm extremely grateful for what you did for me. You of all people must realize, however, that I would be the most sensitive to any attempt to make Demetrius look guilty when you yourself have admitted you have no evidence that he was ever involved with this money-laundering operation. It is because of our previous dealings that I told everyone in the club that you are an honest cop, and that if Demetrius is really innocent of this crime, you would be his best friend in proving it. I told them that you would conduct the investigation with the utmost integrity, but you can't expect me to advise my friends to compromise themselves by talking to you in an active murder investigation without a lawyer present. You of all people should know I would never do that."

I glare at him. "Are you sure that's really the reason?"

He frowns at me. "What other reason would there be?"

"Why did you even let me into the club?" I demand. "I thought you would cooperate with me."

"I am cooperating. I'm cooperating within the bounds of the law. I let you into the club because everyone here has a right to know if Demetrius really was laundering money through this man's criminal organization. We have a right to know if Demetrius is even suspected of laundering money through some criminal organization." He frowns at me. "Now you answer my question. What other reason would there be?"

I hesitate. "I just wondered if it might be because of me."

He understands instantly—which means he was thinking it, too.

He's one of the most attractive guys I've met in a long time—and not just physically. He isn't the most imposing, but he has a quiet kind of self-possession that makes him irresistibly appealing.

He's also a perfect gentleman at all times, a humanitarian, and his manners are always absolutely unimpeachable.

I guess that's the main thing about him. Everything about him is unimpeachable. No one can find any fault with anything he does because he always does everything right.

He's a genuinely good person. Everyone knows it. Everyone defended him when he got accused of murder. No one would believe anything bad about him because he would never do anything bad.

He would treat any woman like a lady even if he never had any plans ever to see her again—or ever to see her in the first place. He stepped in to protect me at the bar when he never had any reason to think anything would ever happen between us.

I don't know if anything would or could ever happen between us after I investigated him for murdering someone in such a horrific way.

I would go out with him, though. The fact that I did investigate him for murdering someone in such a horrific way is exactly the reason I would go out with him. I found out what he's really made of by investigating him.

He takes a deep breath. "Listen to me, Jocelyn. I find you very attractive, but I can't overcome our shared past so easily. You're a Police officer investigating someone I know and do business with. I feel a special responsibility to defend his innocence until he's proven guilty—and I know you feel the same way. I know you would never paint Demetrius into a corner without the evidence to back it up—and I couldn't let you. I hope you can respect that."

"I do respect it—and I do feel the same way." I hesitate a second time. "And I also find you attractive. I just wasn't sure if you were letting that get in the way of what I'm trying to do here."

"I wouldn't do that." Now he's the one who hesitates. "If you find me attractive and I find you attractive, maybe you would like to go out with me."

I blink at him. "Really?"

He shrugs. "If you want to. I promise I won't walk out of the building in the middle of our date."

I should laugh at that, but something stops me. "I would love to go out with you."

"Excellent." He pulls out his phone. "Could I get your number? Oh, wait. I already have it." He laughs at himself.

I can't remember ever seeing him laugh before. He lights up with blushing delight when he realizes his mistake. I can't stop staring at him. He looks like a completely different person from every other time I've seen him. He's always been so serious in the past.

I guess he had good reason to be serious.

His eyes lift to my face and he realizes I'm staring at him like he has three heads. His cheeks color again. "I'll call you tonight and we can arrange a time to go out. Okay?"

"Uh....okay." I realize I'm stammering like a moron. He actually asked me out. He actually joked about it.

He smiles at me. "I also promise we won't talk about any of your cases. Is it a deal?"

"Okay." I shake myself. "I promise I won't turn this into an interrogation session."

He grins at me again. He actually looks even more drop-dead gorgeous when he smiles. He looks genuinely delighted to be going out with me. This is new.

He holds out his hand. "I think you're a wonderful person, Jocelyn. I admire what you do. I would never undermine it. I'm trying to help you as much as possible while maintaining the spirit and integrity of the club and my business relationships. I hope you can understand."

I pull my head out of the clouds enough to shake his hand. "I do understand and I respect that. I'm sorry I went off on you."

"Not at all." He tightens his grip on my hand. He lingers there and doesn't let go for what seems like a long time. "Please feel free to go off on me whenever you please."

I burst into a grin, too, before I think better of it and try to fight it back. "I guess....I guess I'll talk to you tonight."

"Yes, you will." His face glows. Wow. He's really happy about this.

He finally lets go of my hand. "I better go inside before these security guys get ideas."

I can't even look at the security guys. They all just heard him ask me out.

"Bye," I murmur.

"Goodbye, Jocelyn. Have a wonderful day."

I turn around. He doesn't go inside. He stands there watching me walk away. I mercifully get to the street corner and turn off so he can't see me anymore, but I can't help but get butterflies when I think about him.

I'm going out with him. He actually knows what I do and he still wants to go out with me. I can't believe it, but it's real. I just hope he still likes me after the first date—and maybe even beyond.

Chapter 16: Diego

I knock on Jocelyn's door at eight o'clock on Saturday night. I can't help but shuffle my feet like the nervous teenager I am. This is the most excited I've been about a date in a long time.

I know Jocelyn a lot better than most other girls I've gone out with on first dates. I know her too well. That's exactly what makes her so damn appealing.

It isn't her looks even though she's gorgeous in a simple, no-nonsense way. She takes far less pains to pretty herself up than just about every other woman I have ever met. She barely even wears makeup. In fact, I can't remember if she even does wear makeup.

She doesn't need it. It's her heart that makes me so attracted to her—her pure, golden heart. She's so honest, genuine, and good. I can't help but stand in awe of how unbelievably good she is.

I can't think of anyone who would actually track down someone on the other side of a conflict like that murder investigation and deliberately give the other side information to destroy her own position. That took pure, iron guts and bulletproof integrity.

She cares as much or more about doing the right thing as anyone I can think of. She cares about it as much or more than some of the most admirable members of The Billionaires' Club. I absolutely trust her with my life. I would be stupid not to.

I can't think of anyone I've ever met that I trust as much as I trust her. I would be throwing away a priceless treasure if I passed up the opportunity to go out with her.

I don't know if it will work out. Her own integrity makes her hard-headed at times, but I can deal with that. She's always reasonable about it. I can always get through to her if I just explain things in reasonable terms.

She's emotional. She's a woman. I have no problem with that.

She answers the door wearing a simple black dress with a tiered, ruffled skirt. She wears a short, white leather jacket with a ruff of fur around the collar and cuffs. She looks elegant without looking too done up.

I laugh when I see her. "I actually wondered if you would show up wearing your usual black pants and biker jacket."

She blushes at me. "I do own other clothes."

"You look stunning. You always do no matter what you wear." I offer her my arm. "Are you ready?"

"Yeah." She beams at me and slips her hand through my arm.

In that moment, I catch one split-second glimpse into her apartment. It's a humble place. I only get a look into the living room with a hand-sewn patchwork quilt over the couch, a beat-up coffee table, and a TV screen on the wall.

An old, fading velvet pink armchair sits at an angle to the couch. The living room is too small for any other furniture.

I lead her back toward the elevator. "Why do you always wear the same outfit to work?" I ask while we wait for the elevator to come.

"It just makes things so much simpler. I guess I do it to reduce decision fatigue and to save time when I have to decide what I'm going to wear every day. I know some of the women in the department—and even the men—they go through an agony of decision every day and they're always updating their wardrobes so they look their best."

"Don't you want to look your best?"

"Of course. I went through all of that for my first few years on the Force. Then I realized that the people who are seeing me every day aren't going to think any less of me if I dress one way instead of another. They're dealing with an NYPD detective either way. What I wear doesn't change that as long as I come to work well-groomed and look professional. I realized that wearing this outfit every day doesn't make me look any less professional—and it makes a certain impression on people that a business suit or casual clothes can't make. It has kind of become my uniform—my calling card. People expect it and it makes an impression—which is the impression I want to make on people. I don't want them to see me as a businessperson in a suit. I want them to see me as a cop. I want them to see me as....well, I guess it's like this is my superhero identity and the outfit is my costume. It shows everyone that I'm in superhero cop mode and they better not mess with me."

I laugh. "That's an interesting way of putting it."

"Wearing a suit or business attire is generic. It makes a person invisible. I don't want to be either of those things and I don't want people to see me as a business professional who just happens to be a cop. I'm *not* those things. I'm.....well, I'm me. The outfit announces who I am to the world—the version of me that I want to announce to the world."

I find myself beaming at her, but the elevator comes just then and we get into it. I love the feeling of her hand on my arm. She really is beautiful.

"You look outstanding in your superhero outfit," I tell her. "You look every bit as professional—and you do look like a cop. You look like a completely unique version of a cop—and it does make an impression. It makes a very striking impression."

"I know it does. The reactions I get from people tell me exactly the impression I'm making. It's very different from the impression I made in a suit with my hair in a bun and all my makeup and jewelry standing out."

I grin at her. "I can just imagine you like that."

She smirks back at me. "And what impression does that make on you?"

"A very different one than the one I got from your superhero outfit."

"You see? I told you so."

I face front. "I think it's a very good outfit for you. I approve."

She laughs. "Thank you."

"Have any of your superiors or coworkers commented that you look inappropriate?"

"Not at all. They definitely seem to approve."

"I'm not at all surprised. You see? I'm not the only one."

The elevator doors open and I escort her outside to my waiting limo. She slides into the seat and adjusts her position while she waits for me to get in after her. Then she smiles at me again.

"I'm going to have to scratch this off my bucket list—going on a date with a billionaire."

"You aren't going on a date with a billionaire. You're going on a date with me."

"Yeah." She smiles even more broadly. "That's what makes it so good."

"Is going on a date with me so different from going on a date with anyone else?" I ask. "Apart from me being a billionaire, I mean?"

"I know you a lot better than anyone I've ever gone on a first date with before. I mean, I know a lot about you."

I find myself gazing into her eyes. "I was thinking the same thing about you just before when I was waiting for you to come to the door."

She looks away. "Anyway, we agreed not to talk about that."

"When was the last time you went out with someone seriously? Or is that too personal a question to ask?"

"I don't mind. I went out with a guy for five years. That was....well, five years ago. I've gone on the dates I told you about with people who don't want to date a homicide detective. I haven't gone out with anyone seriously since then."

"Tell me what happened. What was the relationship like and how did it end?"

She looks up at me. "Do you really want to know?"

"Of course. I want to know everything about you. Don't you know you fascinate me, Jocelyn? I want to know how you came to be the person that you are."

She looks away again. "The truth is that he was the one who gave me the idea to go to the Police Academy. I graduated from high school with no plans, no training, and my grades weren't good enough for me to get into college. I got a job working as a waitress in a diner on the Lower East Side. We met because he was a construction worker and came into the diner for breakfast every morning. We dated for six months and then moved in together. We actually got engaged and were planning to get married. He decided he wanted to go to the Police Academy so he could get a better job and support the family. I said I wanted to go, too. I didn't want to be a waitress all my life."

"That sounds excellent. I'm proud of you."

She blushes. "Well, he wasn't. He got completely bent out of shape and said he would dump me if I went. He said he didn't want to marry another cop. He wanted me to be there at home cooking and cleaning for him and waiting for him to get home from work. He actually liked the idea of me waiting at home worrying if he would come home at all. I realized he never really loved me. He never wanted anything better for me or for me to have any dreams or aspirations beyond just being a stay-at-home wife for him. I realized he would never support my dreams and aspirations even if I wanted to do something other than being a cop. I decided to test him and I agreed to his demands. I told him I would give up the idea of becoming a cop and I would start an at-home online business instead to help make money for the family. He forbade that, too, exactly the way I knew he would. He said he would dump me if I did. I told him I would do it anyway and he dumped me."

"My God!" I breathe. "What an idiot!"

She laughs. "Do you want to know the craziest part? We both entered the Academy at the same time. We were in the same class. I beat him in every test, every physical agility metric, every shooting range evaluation, every self-defense course, and every written legal exam. He refused to even look at me, not even at graduation. We never spoke even once after we split up."

I cluck my tongue and look away. "You're definitely better off without him."

"I know. That's what I realized."

"I'm glad you got away from him and I'm glad you bettered yourself. You seem to have found your true calling in life."

"Yeah. I did." She beams at me. "I love that you can accept it."

I snort at her. "I would be stupid not to after what you've done for me."

Her eyes soften....and then her eyes dart down to my mouth before she looks away again. "So what made you go into business?"

Now it's my turn to look away and shrug. "My father instilled in all his children the need to constantly improve one's lot in life. He believed in hard work and he modeled it for us. He spent every free moment working on his own projects, side businesses—all of that."

"What was his side business? I know he worked in the diplomatic corps in Spain."

"He was a writer on the side. He ran an online publishing website that launched the careers of unknown authors and short story writers. He sought them out, gave them editorial feedback on their work, and nurtured them to get good enough to publish on his site. He was highly respected in the field. Publishing houses used to patronize his website to find new talent. It was his passion project and he loved it."

"So how did you get into this business of yours?" she asks. "It isn't exactly the same concept, is it?"

"There were a few extremely wealthy individuals there in Madrid where we lived. I always liked their lifestyle and I wanted the luxury that they had. I started out very small-time in business trying to strike it rich so I could have all the nice houses and cars that they had. Then I got a little older and realized that most of these men were mobsters and cutthroats with countless criminal convictions and suspected in many more crimes they had never been caught for. They got away with most of it by paying off the law enforcement agencies or simply by bumping off anyone upstanding enough to go after them."

She laughs. "Ouch."

"Exactly. My father was an extremely law-abiding man. I knew he would probably disown me if he ever found out I did anything illegal. I grew up desperately craving his approval and for him to be proud of me for my accomplishments. It took me many years to understand that I could be successful in business without compromising my integrity or his standards."

"How did you finally make the connection?"

"I met a few very wealthy European businessmen who made their money legitimately. I decided to copy them instead and it worked."

"So does your father approve of you? Is he proud of you?"

"He died before I became successful, so he never found out that I attained this level of wealth. He died believing that I'm a law-abiding citizen who genuinely believes in doing the right thing for others. That's what matters—that he died with the right impression of me and that I continue to maintain that standard to this day. I know he would approve of me if he had lived long enough to find out."

She gazes at me across the seat. "That's an amazing story. I'm proud of you for bettering yourself, too, and I wholeheartedly approve of your personal ethic. It's the one thing that made me want to go out with you. I never thought a billionaire could be as good as you, but you showed me the light."

I can't help but grin at her, but the limo pulls up at the restaurant just then and we get out to go inside.

I offer her my arm again and she grins when she takes it. We both know we're on a date and we both act like it. This feels good. I love her company. She's magnetic and yet so easy to talk to and get along with. I love sharing ideas and stories with her.

Chapter 17: Diego

Jocelyn and I walk into a luxurious restaurant full of glittering crystal chandeliers, silver cutlery, waiters in tuxedoes, and almost everyone in here is dressed in eveningwear.

I'm not wearing a tux and she isn't wearing an evening gown, but we both fit in. No one looks sideways at either of us.

Jocelyn doesn't act at all uncomfortable about walking into this place on my arm. She acts completely relaxed and at ease with herself. She would act completely relaxed and at ease even at a Billionaires' Club gala. She has nothing to prove to anyone or herself.

She doesn't balk when I pull out her chair for her to sit down. I sit down opposite her and she gives me the most brilliant smile. We're on a date. The surroundings don't distract her from that.

"Hi," she murmurs.

"Hello, there. Fancy meeting you here."

She giggles. "So what do you want to talk about next?"

"Anything but your cases."

"What is it like being a billionaire? How do you think it compares to being a non-billionaire?"

I shrug. "It's very much the same. I still go to the bathroom at times."

She laughs. "I didn't mean that part."

"My house is bigger. My car is bigger. My company is bigger, but other than that, it isn't that much different. It does nothing to shield me from being accused of murder, for example."

She grimaces. "We aren't talking about that, either."

"The folks in the club are a much higher caliber of social acquaintance. I suppose that's the biggest difference. When I walk into the club, I don't have to worry if one of them is going to decide that anyone over a certain net worth should be rounded up and held in a concentration camp. So that's a relief."

"Has anyone ever walked out on a date when they found out what you do? Did *she* ever find out what you do?"

"She didn't find out until I explained to her why I didn't want to go on a second date. That's when I told her. Most people want to date me *because* they know what I do. You have to stop people from going out with you at this level. You have to stop the people who want to go out with you for that reason and only because of that reason."

Her smile evaporates. "Does that happen a lot?"

"All the time. Every man in the club has gone through the same thing. Certain people go along with it. Certain people who will remain unnamed let these others throw themselves at us so they can enjoy themselves." I raise my hands. "No judgment on them. Each to their own. I don't do that, though. I have better things to do."

"So when was the last time you dated someone seriously?"

"I had a fiancé in Spain—like you. We got together when I had nothing. We were together for six years from the time I graduated from high school until I moved to the US. I moved here because she broke up with me."

"Why did she break up with you?"

"I was mid-level then. I was making enough to support myself and her. I wasn't doing too badly, but I wasn't rich, either. I couldn't give her any luxury gifts or anything like that. We were solidly, comfortably middle-class, but I was improving. I was building and expanding my business all the time. She went on a holiday with her family to Majorca and met some rich playboy there. She ran off with him and told me I would always be a mid-level player and never get anywhere in life. She said I was nothing and she could do better."

"Wow. That's awful."

"She actually did me a great favor. I wouldn't have moved to New York if not for her. I would have stayed with her and I probably would have always stayed a mid-level player like she said. Maybe that's why she did it—because that's what she saw in our future together. Anyway, I moved to New York because of the breakup—to get away from it. My business expanded once I got around better contacts and more people who played at a higher level than me. I met some members of The Billionaires' Club and they helped me by giving me their business. It all went from there."

"What made you decide to move here? Was it only the breakup? Did you come here sight unseen or was there something else that made you decide?"

"My father died shortly before this all happened. His parents contacted me and my siblings after his death and offered for any of us to come over and live with them—to find out how the other half of the family lived. We all grew up in Spain. None of us had ever set foot in America. My older brother and I both came. My grandparents lived in Queens, so it turned out to be the perfect place for me. All my business contacts were in Europe and the Middle East. I wasn't sure how I would continue my business here, but it worked out for the best and all my previous experience worked in my favor. I was able to connect my new contacts here with people I had done business with over there. It was the perfect solution. Later I found out that my former fiancé spent a total of two weeks with her new boyfriend. Then he dumped her and she went back to Madrid alone, so I came out the winner."

She beams at me. "That's awesome. Congratulations."

"I can't complain, can I?"

The waiter comes just then and Jocelyn and I both order. I extend my hand to her after he leaves. She takes it and blushes.

Her hand feels soft and warm. That's the thing about her. I know she's a cop and a damn good one. She could probably kick my ass, but she's so soft and receptive. She's all woman when she's with me.

She blushes again when she sees me looking at her. "I don't even want to know what you're thinking right now," she tells me.

"I'm thinking this is the nicest date I've ever been on—bar none."

Her eyelashes dip and she turns bright red. "Me, too. You're an excellent date."

"Is your family in New York?" I ask. "Are you from around here?"

"I have a brother who lives in Brooklyn and a sister who lives in Puerto Rico. They both have families. The rest of my relatives are all gone now."

"I'm sorry to hear that."

She shrugs. "That's the way it goes, I guess. What about your siblings? Where are they?"

"My older brother is a businessman in Queens and lives near where my grandparents used to live. He's a perpetual bachelor and doesn't have a family. My younger brother got involved with the aforementioned cutthroats and met an untimely death at the age of twenty-six. My sister lives in Madrid with her husband and children. She's a stay-at-home wife like your former fiancé wanted you to be. My sister doesn't speak to me or my older brother."

She frowns. "Why not?"

"I have no idea. She doesn't call us and we don't call her. My older brother called her once about a year after we moved here. She ranted to him about how he and I betrayed our family by moving to the US. He tried to explain it to me afterward, but she was so irate that he didn't really understand her reasoning himself. He told her he wouldn't call again, that he would always wait for her to call him, and that he and I would always be there for her if she ever needed us or wanted to reconnect. She hasn't. That's the last we've heard from her."

"How bizarre. I wonder why she got that idea."

"I'm not sure. I suppose I could have called her to find out for myself or if she has softened her idea since then, but I somehow continue not to call. I once mentioned it to my brother and he told me not to. He said that she was the one who betrayed our family by pushing us away as she did—simply for the crime of moving to another country to meet the other side of our family. He said she wouldn't have been able to make the same claim if we moved to France or England, for example. He said he would demand an apology if she ever called him and he wouldn't speak to her unless she did apologize. I suppose I never felt strongly enough about it one way or the other to cross that bridge. He's the one relative I still have left alive. I wouldn't want him to think I betrayed him by establishing communication with her when he felt so strongly opposed to it."

She raises her eyebrows. "I guess I can't argue with that."

"Are you close to your brother's family?"

"I see them every now and then. I wouldn't say we're close."

"What did they think of you becoming a cop? What did your brother think of it?"

She shrugs. "He was neutral about it. He still is. He didn't approve or disapprove. He didn't approve or disapprove of me becoming anything better than a waitress. It was kind of like he didn't really care what I did. I'm his little sister. That isn't part of it for him—which I can deal with. We're family no matter what my job is. He's going to feel the same way about me no matter what I do—and it's almost like he'll always consider me the same person no matter what. If I improve my circumstances or let's say for example if I decided to go back to college and become a rocket scientist, he wouldn't really care. I'll still be his little sister and he'll still have the same opinion of me—which I suppose is a good thing. I mean—isn't that what family is—that they always accept you no matter what? That's the way I see it. That's the way I understand his attitude toward me. Us being family isn't mutable or dependent on anything or conditional on anything. It's eternal—like gravity. It doesn't change with times and conditions, good or bad."

I find myself beaming at her again. "I love that. That is so beautiful that you see it that way."

The waiter comes just then to deliver our food and we start eating. I don't stop looking at her across the table while we eat and I sure as hell don't stop holding her hand.

I love that we can talk so freely about these things. I love that she feels so open to talk to me about everything going on in her head and in her heart. She holds nothing back.

She explains things so clearly and openly. I've never met anyone like her. I really feel like I'm falling head over heels for her.

I can't wait to go even deeper. I can't wait to find out all the new things she might be hiding beneath the surface.

Chapter 18: Jocelyn

Diego holds my hand when I slide into the back of his limo. Riding around in a limo with him feels like I'm some kind of celebrity. I feel like I'm living some kind of TV show about the lifestyles of the rich and infamous.

He gets in next to me and we both make eye contact, grin, and blush at each other. I love how excited he is by this whole thing. He doesn't play it off like this is all ho-hum and ordinary to him. He actually makes me feel like this date is a special treat for him.

It's a special treat for me, too. I've never connected with anyone on a date like this. He's a special guy and he treats me like I'm special to him, too. That's what makes it so good.

The limo pulls away and glides into traffic. He doesn't mention taking me anywhere but home. He doesn't mention us going home to one of our houses or hooking up or anything like that.

He really plans to just drop me off like the gentleman he is. He doesn't want to take it any further than that—because he respects me. He doesn't want to insult me by suggesting that we bang each other on the very first date.

He turns to me in the car. "I had a wonderful time tonight, Jocelyn. I would love to take you out again sometime—as long as you don't want to put me in a concentration camp."

I laugh. "I don't—and congratulations on getting through the date without walking out on me."

"I would tell you if I didn't want to see you again." His eyes dip to my mouth. "I definitely want to see you again."

The chemistry between us escalates the minute he says that. His eyes and expression communicate all the emotion and potential we've both been feeling since he asked me out. Our time together means so much more than it ever did when we kept it professional.

He leans forward and towers over me, but he doesn't kiss me—not yet. I look up and down between his eyes and his mouth. He's going to kiss me. He just holds off—long enough to light me on fire.

I really want to kiss him. I want to feel what he feels like when he kisses a woman he wants.

He wants me. I see that in his eyes and in the way he acts toward me. He acts like he wants me a lot. He doesn't hold me at a distance—not ever.

My heart skips a beat when I feel him so near me. Just thinking about him kissing me brings up so many fevered imaginations about his hands all over my body—about my hands all over his body—our clothes coming off....

I get a mental flash of what he might look like with his clothes off....and then his lips touch mine. Our eyes drift shut in the deep, sultry, silken wetness of his tongue swirling through my lips.

He kisses passionately and wholeheartedly. He holds nothing back. He leans against me and lets me feel the tension pulsing through his muscles. His tongue coils around mine in a sensual, suggestive ripple of pure erotic madness.

I circle my arms around his neck and fall back on the seat. He leans his weight all the way over me and his hands start exploring my body the way I imagined—but only almost just barely getting to the level of heat I dream about.

He doesn't touch my breasts or weasel his hands between my legs or grab my ass or any of that. He stops just short of that to make me want him even more.

His touch spirals me out of control, but I can't cross that line. He lets me feel him starting to get hard, but he doesn't take it any further than that. He doesn't grind into me or get between my legs, not even when I raise one leg next to his hip.

He pulls me tight against him, but that's all. Our bodies move in a soft, blissful ripple of delicious desire. It's enough that we both feel this pulsating desire for each other. That's all this is. It isn't about slamming into each other only to go our separate ways afterward.

My desire for him feels amazing. I love just being here with him in how we both feel about each other. I love that neither of us needs it to be something more than this.

It will become more if we keep going like this. We'll get to know each other, but we'll never find out anything that makes us dislike or lose respect for each other. That isn't possible.

I would get together with him right now if I had to choose. I would get into a long-term relationship with him just based on what I know about him right now. I might even marry him just based on what I know about him right now.

I won't find out anything damning or anything bad at all. I'm certain of it. He's good to the bottom of his soul. No one can convince me otherwise.

I've already found that out about him. I've found out as much as all those people who have known him for years. They already know him so much better than I do and they were willing to defend him when he was accused of premeditated murder.

They knew he couldn't have done it. It never once crossed their minds that he could be guilty of something like that. Now I know why. It's ridiculous when I think about it.

He leans a little farther forward and swings his legs up onto the seat. He lies all the way down on top of me, but he still doesn't escalate.

This is actually so comfortable. I can imagine us lying together like this on a couch in our own living room. It's like we're a married couple relaxing together and neither of us feels like going any further than just lying here together.

My eyes float open and so do his. We stare into each other's eyes—and I see the same truth all the way down there at the bottom of his soul. He's thinking the same thing. We don't have to take it further because we're already there.

Then, for no reason at all, we both start laughing. He makes me happy and I can see that I make him happy.

He pulls off from kissing me and beams down at me. "Am I to understand from this that you will definitely go out with me a second time?" he asks.

"Maybe one more time." I laugh again. "Okay, maybe twice more."

He laughs back at me. "That's good. I like going out with you."

"I like going out with you, too. This feels comfortable and solid."

He sits up on the seat, takes my hand, and pulls me to lift me upright. He doesn't let go of my hand and he doesn't stop smirking at me in excited happiness. "Can I call you?" he asks. "I mean, can I call you for no reason other than just because I want to talk to you?"

"You can call me whenever you want to. You should know that. I would always love to hear from you."

He blushes and winds up laughing. "Excellent. I'm pleased."

The limo pulls up in front of my apartment building and he walks me inside. We hold hands in the elevator riding up and all the way down the hall to my apartment. We stop outside the door.

His eyes sparkle when he looks at me. "Good night, Jocelyn," he murmurs between smirks.

"Good night, Diego. You're not going to turn this all formal, are you?"

"Do you mean like this?" He takes a step back, does a sweeping flourish of a bow, and kisses my hand. "Fare thee well, oh benighted fair lady....."

I burst out laughing. "Stop it! Do you even know what, 'benighted' means?"

"Doesn't it mean shadowy and mysterious?"

"No! It means backward, ignorant, stupid, and uncultured."

Now he's the one who laughs. "Oops. Okay, scratch that." He raises his other hand like he's giving a Shakespearean speech. "Fare thee well, oh shadowy and mysterious fair lady...."

I wipe away tears of laughter. "Okay. I think it's time for you to get the hell out of here before you make a complete fool of yourself."

He straightens up and grins at me. "Good night, Jocelyn. You are such a fun date. I'll call you about when we can go out again."

"Okay. Good night. I had a really nice time tonight. I'll talk to you this week."

He leans in and kisses me before he pulls away and lets our fingers slip apart. He points toward the apartment. "You better go change into your superhero identity."

I laugh. "Bye."

"Bye." He walks off around the corner toward the elevator. I unlock my apartment and go inside. He makes me happy. I love going out with him. I can't wait for him to call me so we can talk during the week. It's going to be great.

Chapter 19: Diego

I get out of the limo and head for The Billionaires' Club for our weekly meeting. We call it a meeting, but it's really just a social gathering where we hang out and talk.

I make it halfway to the entrance when I get a phone call. It's from Jocelyn.

"Don't you have some bad guys to catch?" I tease when I answer the phone.

"That's what I want to talk to you about. I was wondering if you could get me back into the club again so I can question a few more people about Demetrius Runyon."

"Um.....I suppose I could do that. We're having a meeting in half an hour. You could come now if you want to."

"Really? Will he be there?"

"I don't know if he'll be here, but you could come and talk to other people if you really want to."

"That would be great. Are you okay with that? I don't want to put you in a compromising position."

"Please, Jocelyn," I tell her. "I'm not compromising myself. I'm reciprocating by helping you a tiny fraction of how much you helped me. If Demetrius is innocent, then you coming to the club will only help you find that out, won't it?"

"The others might not see it that way."

"I see it that way—and in any case, I'm doing you a favor to recip-rocate. Now get off the phone and come down here. I'll be inside. The guards will call me to tell me when you arrive. I'll come out and escort you in."

"Thank you. I'll see you in a few minutes."

She hangs up and I go inside. A bunch of people are here, but Demetrius isn't.

"Jocelyn is coming by again," I tell them. "She wants to interview us about the Pinkerton investigation."

"Is that really necessary, Diego?" Rory asks. "Is it really necessary that she come to interview us here? We come here to relax together away from people like her. We come here to spend time with each other—not to get interviewed by the Police."

"She's a homicide detective carrying out her duties in the service of law and order," I tell him. "I'm sure she can interview each of us separately outside of the club just as easily, Would you really prefer it if she showed up to interview you at your place of business where everyone will see you giving a statement to the Police in connection with a homicide investigation? None of us is under suspicion for this crime. It would look absolutely terrible if each of us lawyered up and refused to speak to her. I personally would rather answer her questions here where she's questioning all of you at the same time. I wouldn't want her showing up at my office or anywhere else she happened to find me."

He shrugs and doesn't bring it up again.

"I told you all before," I go on. "Jocelyn is an honest cop and a good person. She believes in the law. She won't do anything to un-derhandedly implicate anyone unless she has hard evidence to indicate their guilt. Someone is using a company name in connection with the

Billionaires' Club to launder money through a criminal organization. We should all be extremely interested in clearing up this matter and finding out who the person is. I don't know about you, but I plan to cooperate with Jocelyn's investigation and tell her whatever it is she wants to know. I won't tell her anything about what I know about the murder—which is nothing. I can give her plenty of information without doing that. I would do the same for any person off the street who walked into the Halcyon building and asked me about my dealings. I certainly wouldn't hide it."

"You're right, Diego," Dante tells me. "We would all do the same thing. I would consider it extremely shady if someone did anything else."

"Exactly." I get a phone call just then. "She's outside. I'll go get her."

I meet up with Jocelyn outside. She smiles at me and then her smile drains when she sees the security guards. "How is it going up there?"

"I've softened them up for you. They're expecting you and they plan to cooperate with your investigation. Just don't ask about the murder or Demetrius's involvement in it. These people don't know anything about it anyway."

She nods. "Is he up there?"

"No, he isn't. He may come later, but he isn't there now."

I lead her upstairs. The guys act much more casual about her being here.

I take her back to the main group where Jackson, Dante, Lane, Judah, Giovanni, Kevin, and Derek stand in a cluster.

"Thank you gentlemen for seeing me," she begins.

"What would you like to know, Detective?" Jackson asks. "We'll tell you whatever you want to know—as long as you understand that none of us can tell you about the murder. None of us knew about it until you told us."

"I understand that. I want to ask you all about your dealings with Spiderware."

"My company does business with Spiderware," I tell her. "We do business with Spiderware all the time."

"So does mine," Kevin adds. "I mean....Paige's does. SigmaTech has started integrating Spiderware systems into their new prototype line. Paige does business with Demetrius all the time—and my company has started running Spiderware training programs. So yeah, I work with Demetrius."

"What can you two tell me about him? Do either of you know him well?"

"I only know him in business," I tell her. "I don't know him personally. I don't usually socialize with him outside the club."

"He hasn't been in the club that long," Kevin points out. "He comes to weekly meetings and galas, but that's about it. We all hang out together in our personal lives, but I guess you could say he just hasn't gotten to know us well enough—or maybe he has his own thing going. I don't know."

She frowns at him. "What's a gala?"

"We hold gala events four times a year," I tell her. "They're black-tie evenings—usually held at the Four Seasons Hotel ballroom or some other luxury venue like that. It's just another environment where we get together to spend time with each other."

"What's the difference?" she asks. "Why do you do that when you could just spend time with each other here?"

"We can all bring our wives and dates to the galas," Dante tells her. "They aren't allowed here. The club is members only—so the only wives and dates who are allowed through the door have to be other billionaires—like Paige and Melody Gottlieb. That's the only reason you see women here—if they're billionaire club members. Members are invited to bring a guest to the galas. It can be anyone. It doesn't have to be another member. Our wives and girlfriends and other dates can get together socially at the galas. We can all get together there in ways we can't otherwise. See?"

"Oh, okay. I understand." She glances around. "So does any of you know Demetrius socially? Does he ever bring a wife, girlfriend, or other date to the galas?"

"No, he never does," I tell her. "He always comes alone. I always assumed he was single, but maybe his wife or girlfriend doesn't want to come. Maybe she doesn't know the other women well enough to want to come."

"How would she get to know them if she didn't come?" she asks.

"That's the whole point," Jackson tells her. "That's one of the first places a new person gets to know everyone—at the galas. They get acquainted and then they feel comfortable getting together outside of that context. That's the way it usually works." He turns to Giovanni. "That's how it happened for Mila, isn't it? It happens that way for almost all of them—and I suppose it happens for the female billionaires' husbands, too, doesn't it? They wouldn't be able to meet us anywhere else."

"I see," Jocelyn replies. "Do any of you know anything about Demetrius's background—where he came from, where he lived before this, what he did to make his money—anything like that?"

"You would have to ask him that," I tell her. "He hasn't told us—or he hasn't told me." I turn to the others. "Have any of you talked to him about that?"

They all shake their heads. "He's kind of a private, guarded kind of guy," Derek remarks. "He gives you the impression that he doesn't want to talk about his personal life. He always has plenty to say about business. He always has a tendency to steer the conversation back to that. I got the impression not to ask."

"I got the same feeling," I tell him.

She turns to me. "What kind of business do you do with him?"

"I broker the sale and adoption of his software to militaries and government organizations around the world. I have contacts in several international militaries, including some that no one else deals with. I've sold them food supplies, electronics, medical supplies, brokered personnel training programs through Kevin's organization—that kind of thing. I do large contacts and brokerages between multinational corporations and governments and militaries. That's my specialty. So Demetrius comes to me and lets me know if he wants me to approach a certain organization or government department of a certain country to make a bid or proposal for his systems and software or I may approach him on behalf of one of these departments or organizations or if I see a good fit for the two. Then we negotiate from there."

"Have you done many deals with him?"

"Five in total so far. One was with the Pentagon. One was with the Chinese space exploration department. The third was with the British Parliament. The fourth was with a multinational aviation company, but I can't tell you which one because the deal was covered by a non-disclosure agreement. The fifth was with SigmaTech, Paige Novak's medical equipment company to use Spiderware in her research and development program."

Jocelyn nods at me. "Okay. Thank you for being so forthcoming about this."

I spread my hands. "I don't see that you'll be able to use this information in your investigation. Those deals were all completely above board. I wouldn't have gotten involved in them at all if I had known any of the funds would go to some sleazy money-laundering outfit downtown."

"I know you wouldn't. I was just trying to gauge how much you knew about Demetrius."

"I can tell you about his business—at least as far as it intersects with mine. That's all I can tell you. What he does with his money is outside my purview."

I become aware of everyone else in the room standing around listening in silence. They hear me answering all her questions. I have nothing to hide from her. Maybe if they see me opening up to her, they'll do the same thing.

For just a minute, I can convince myself that she and I are alone in the room. I feel the way I did at the restaurant. We're talking to each other openly, honestly, with no defenses or hidden agendas.

She gazes back into my eyes as clearly as she did that night. She doesn't seem to notice everyone else around us. Her steady gaze enhances the illusion that we're alone together and I'm confiding in her.

I trust her with this information. I know she'll use it appropriately. I have nothing to fear from her.

She turns away from me, but not because the silence makes her uncomfortable. She glances around the circle. "What about the rest of you? What about you, Mr. Drake? What were your dealings with Demetrius Runyon?"

"My dealings with him were also strictly professional," Kevin replies. "The deal he did with SigmaTech required me to run training programs between his people and SigmaTech people to train them on how to use his software. He sent his people over to train a series of trainers who would then pass the information on to another batch of SigmaTech people who would actually use the software. So it became an assembly line of training, trainers, and trainees if you see what I mean." He laughs at the combination of words.

Jocelyn grins at him and snickers, too. "I get it. So People, Inc. coordinated all of the training, trainers, and trainees."

"Yeah. That's right."

She surveys the rest of the men standing around. "Can any of you shed any more light on this for me?"

"Sorry," Jackson tells her. "I've never done business with Demetrius. My business doesn't intersect with his."

"Not many of ours do," Giovanni adds. "Sorry, Detective."

"We probably wouldn't be able to tell you much even if they did intersect," Derek chimes in. "He keeps his personal life to himself. He doesn't reveal anything."

"Okay. I really appreciate you gentlemen taking the time to talk to me," she exclaims. "I wouldn't intrude on your time here if I didn't have an investigation to run—and I will definitely follow up and talk to Demetrius about this."

"You're welcome, Detective," Kevin tells her. "Let us know if we can help you with anything else."

She smiles at them and I follow her outside. I head down the sidewalk to walk her back to her car.

"How did that go?" I ask on the way.

She smiles at me. "Thank you for smoothing things over—and thank you for telling me as much as you did. It definitely made it easier for the others to do the same thing."

"Are you going back to work now?"

She takes a step closer to me. "I want to ask you a favor, Diego."

"Anything. Name it."

"Don't say that until you hear what it is. You might not like it. You might be really offended that I would even ask."

"Okay. Thank you for the warning. Now tell me what it is. Then I'll decide if I'll do it, but I promise not to be offended that you asked. I'll be offended if you *don't* ask."

"I was wondering if you would be willing to take me to the next Billionaires' Club gala as your date. I would like to talk to these people in another context when more of them are around and where I can see Demetrius in action."

I frown at her. "What will that tell you about his involvement in this case?" I raise my hand and shut my eyes. "Wait a minute. You wouldn't be looking into him this deeply if you didn't have reason to believe he really was involved in this murder. Would you?"

She winces. "I don't think I should tell you anything else about the case. I don't think I should tell you why I'm interested in Demetrius."

I compress my lips and narrow my eyes at her. Of course. She must be finding a trail of clues that points to Demetrius as a suspect. I knew it. She would have dropped this line of inquiry if she really thought someone else was using the Spiderware name.

I make a quick decision. Taking her on a date to the gala would be a no-brainer. I would take her on a date anywhere.

"All right. I'll take you," I tell her. "Do you have something to wear? I could take you shopping for an appropriate dress if you like."

She bursts into one of her brilliant smiles. "I would love that."

"The next gala is two weeks from now. I'll take you shopping on Saturday. Will that work?"

"I would love to. Thank you."

I step forward and give her a quick kiss. I catch her blushing at me. "I can't wait to see you all dressed up," I tell her. "You're going to look delicious."

She giggles and makes a run for her car. "Call me, okay?"

"Of course. I'll be dreaming of you until then."

Chapter 20: Jocelyn

I stand in front of my full-length bedroom mirror and look at myself in a long, shimmering gown of dark beige satin. The dress trails on the floor even though I'm wearing tall black, strappy heels underneath.

The slit in the back comes up to my knees—just enough to give me room to walk and show a hint of my shoes when I take a step.

I wear one front lock of my hair pinned back and the rest down. Diego took me shopping to buy me this dress. He couldn't keep his eyes off me when I tried it on and modeled it for him.

He also bought me some jewelry to go with it, but fortunately for my sanity, he bought it when I wasn't around so I didn't see how much it cost. He gave it to me on our last dinner date so I would have it for tonight.

The necklace is a long gold chain with a teardrop diamond set in gold. The long, diamond-studded drape earrings swing and catch the light when I move my head.

He also bought me a magnificent matching diamond bracelet that slithers over my hand every time I put my arm down. All this expensive luxury maintains the illusion that I'm a celebrity in a fantasy world.

I don't look like the kind of person who would live in this dumpy apartment. I definitely don't look like a New York homicide detective. I look like some kind of movie star. I don't recognize myself.

A knock on the door startles me back to my senses. It's time.

I grab my phone and keys and put them in my purse. I have to strut like a model on the catwalk to balance in these heels and this body-hugging dress. They make me feel sultry and seductive in a glamorous, extravagant way.

Diego's eyes widen when I open the door and he sees me. "Holy Mother of God!" he breathes. "I think I may have died and gone to Heaven."

I turn bright red and walk out of the apartment. I see myself sashaying in front of him in ways that make his eyes rivet to my body. "Blink twice if you're ready to go," I tell him.

He blinks twice and we both laugh. He tears his eyes away, pretends to look all the way in the opposite direction, and mumbles, "Pay no attention to that man behind the curtain."

I take his arm and we head for the elevator. I have to walk more slowly than usual so I don't fall over in my heels. Diego doesn't seem in too big a hurry to get there. He keeps casting fleeting glances at me, looking away, and biting back the same thrilled smirk.

"What?" I demand.

"Nothing," he breezes. "Not a thing. Nothing to see here." He stops in front of the elevator and presses the button.

"You're the one who bought the dress," I point out. "And the jewelry...and the shoes."

"Did I?" He pretends to raise his eyebrows at me and immediately has to look away again. His cheeks won't stop coloring every time our eyes meet. "Oh, right. I think I remember now."

I elbow him. "Stop it."

We both step into the elevator and he presses the button to take us to the ground floor. He smirks again when I have to strut into the elevator and take my place at his side.

"You're going to make it extremely difficult for me to keep my hands off you tonight, Jocelyn," he murmurs out the side of his mouth on the way down.

"I'm sure you'll find a way to control yourself."

He turns to face me and his eyes burn into my soul from a few inches away. "I don't want to control myself," he breathes. "I want to lose control with you."

My breath catches when I feel him standing this close to me. This dress makes me feel impossibly sexy. Just wearing it and walking around in it turns me on.

I feel like I want a man to paw me all over my body, take me in the filthiest ways possible, and make me scream like an animal.

Diego's features smolder with the same insane passion. He's the one I want to do that to me. I want him to claw this dress off me, hold me down, and make me lose control, too. I want him to do it right this instant.

His body throbs with buried tension. It radiates into me through his clothes. He's standing near enough to burn me with his intensity. I can't stand to be this far away from him—not for another second.

I want him to strip me, expose me, torment me, and attack me. I start to ache between my legs when I feel him this close. I can't stand the way he makes me feel.

I struggle to breathe....and right then, he threads his fingers into mine. Our hands lock in a moment of deep connection. His eyes hypnotize me into an erotic trance. I feel like I'm doing it with him right this minute.

I need him. I need him all over me and for me to be all over him.

The elevator doors open just then. Four people stand in the building lobby waiting to go upstairs to their own apartments. Diego turns around, untangles our hands from each other, places my hand inside his elbow, and leads me out to the limo waiting at the curb.

He opens the door and holds my hand to help me balance while I get into the car. Every move slithers the dress against my bare skin and my thighs against each other under the dress. That feeling makes me so wet I can't stand it.

Sitting in my wet panties electrifies me even more. I feel slutty and shameless—but at the same time, I feel elegant, exquisite, classy, and almost regal. Diego makes me feel that way.

He sits down next to me. He would always treat me like a lady—right up until the moment when he wouldn't anymore. He wouldn't treat me like a lady if we lost control with each other. Then he would treat me like I was his—the woman who belongs to him.

He adjusts his position on the seat and waits for the car to pull away from the curb. We glide out into traffic—and he turns to look at me.

I didn't realize until now that he was sitting this close to me. The same energy erupts off him and scorches me from inches away. He's thinking that again. He's thinking how much this outfit makes him want his hands all over me—and his body all over me.

Our eyes meet in a moment of pure volcanic madness. He wants to lose control with me and I want to lose control with him. He leans closer, kisses me, and his fingers twine in my hair.

His lips light me up. This doesn't feel comfortable, easy, or timeless the way it did last time. This is unchained fire erupting between us as never before.

Neither of us has ever let go like this before. Neither of us has ever let go at all.

He kisses much harder, faster, hotter, and deeper. He drives in, crushes my mouth under his, and his hand appears on my outer thigh.

I'm wearing a lot fewer clothes this time, too. My breasts press through the thin fabric of my dress and brush his jacket. My bra does nothing to protect me from that extra stimulation.

He slides his hand up my leg and my dress rides up with it. He doesn't try to stop it. He pushes it up and his bare hand lands on the skin of my leg.

I gasp out in the rush of heat at his touch. He pulls off my mouth and stares into my eyes as he pushes my dress up to my hips. Is he going to undress me right here in his limo?

He reacts much faster than I'm ready for, scoops his arms behind me, and lifts me to straddle his lap facing him. This position turns me on beyond belief and I feel him getting hard underneath me.

He strokes his hands up my thighs while we kiss in that position, but he always comes back to pulling away so he can gaze up at me.

I don't tell him to keep his hands to himself. I don't want him to. I want him to slide up my sides and down my hips. We don't have to do anything because this energy between us feels completely different now.

He kisses me deeply and his hands come to rest on my breasts through my sheer gown. His touch skyrockets me into so much desire. I find myself grinding and corkscrewing on his hips to wind up myself up to the highest heights.

He flattens his hand on the small of my back to pull me into his hardness. We're both breathing too fast to talk. He pumps me down on him and I buck and rock on him like we really are doing it.

My mind shuts down in the intoxicating dark power of his eyes. He sends me reeling into a delicious trance feeling like we're already doing it right here in the back of his limo.

He pulls off my mouth, dives into my chest, and crawls his mouth down my neck getting perilously close to my cleavage. I moan and sob—but my world comes crashing down around my ears when he rakes one of my thin dress strap off my shoulder.

That feeling of him exposing me blasts my mind apart. I shudder from the sheer power of how much he makes me want him. I need him to take me right now—right this minute.

He doesn't, though. He leaves blistering kisses down my neck and chest, pulls my bra down, and his mouth clamps on my breast while he paws at the other one.

I rear upright trying to get as much of that sensation as I can. His mouth consumes me with so much heat and exhilarating torment. I grab his head and fail to stop myself from messing up his hair.

He grips me behind my ass and pulls me into his rocking thrusts. I moan in agony. His hard knob excites me so much. Every thrust and squeeze drives my saturated panties aside so I'm sitting right down on his lap.

The limo pulls up in front of the hotel while we're still kissing, panting into each other's mouths, and grinding on each other. Diego lets out tiny little pants of air every time I buck my hips against his tool.

He pulls away again and stares up at me in glazed madness. His features wrench from the strain of holding back the hurricane he wants to unleash on me. No one has to tell me. I feel it already.

He leans back in the seat admiring my face, hair, jewelry, and stroking his warm hands all over my bare skin.

He watches me tremble and shiver when he passes his palms extra lightly over my nipples. Then he strokes down my naked sides and slowly, effortlessly, excruciatingly slides my bra up.

I quake in front of him. It will be like this when we actually do it. I have no shame about my body when he looks at me like this. He looks and feels fantastic. He looks like he really can't wait to get his hands on me.

"Do you feel that?" He digs his hardness into me from below. "This is what I think of the way you look tonight."

I lift off him slightly and slide my hand down between his thighs to play with him. His eyes roll back in their sockets and his features spasm out of control. "Oh, my God, baby!" he whispers. "Yes! Don't stop! I need that so bad!"

He plunges into my neck, but he doesn't kiss me. He closes his arms around me, hides his eyes against my neck, and lets me stroke him to raging hardness. His breath comes out in rasping, panting gasps.

I love the way he sounds like this. I want to unzip his fly and touch him with my bare hand, but he draws away too fast, sits up, and pulls my hand away. "Not yet," he breathes. "Soon....very soon....."

I fall against him kissing him for the stars. He strokes his hands down my back, over my bare shoulders, plays with my breasts until I moan again, and trails his fingertips up my thighs coming dangerously close to my soaked panties.

I might as well not be wearing any panties tonight. He's already scraped them aside and I've already gotten my juices all over his suit. We can't go much further without going all the way.

He finally leans in, kisses me in full, open-mouthed passion, and uses his powerful arms to lift me off him onto the seat next to him.

He smiles at me while he straightens my bra, pulls my dress strap up to cover me, and eases my skirts down. We smile at each other while he straightens my clothes for me. The body underneath this dress already belongs to him and we both know it.

This dress is the wrapping of a present he gave to himself. All he has to do is unwrap it and enjoy the treasure inside.

I see that every time he looks at me. His pupils dilate just a little bit and his gaze traces my curves, down my cleavage, to the slit in my dress where he can see my legs.

He gets out of the limo first and offers me his hand. I need it in these heels.

All trace of what we just did vanishes out of existence when we get out of the car. The light coming from the hotel casts a different halo over us. We're back to being celebrities—royalty.

I slide my hand through Diego's elbow and we strut into the lobby. I feel like a million bucks—or a billion.

Diego smiles at me. His eyes don't dip to my body—not here. That's just between us.

We cross the lobby and enter the grand ballroom. It's already full of men and women in stunning eveningwear—and I'm one of them. We're back with The Billionaires' Club in all its finest.

Chapter 21: Diego

All eyes turn to me and Jocelyn when I lead her into the ballroom gala. The whole club is here—including Demetrius Runyon. No one can stop staring at Jocelyn. Now they all know I brought her here as my date. The cat is out of the bag.

She shines with so much light and beauty. She glows with all the magnetic sex appeal that just made me so dizzy for her in the back of the limo.

I could have done it with her there. I really wanted to. She intoxicates me. I find it difficult to think straight when I touch her like that—and when she touches me like that.

She smiles up at me—but no one can see anything inappropriate about her behavior. She fits right in here. She hovers on my arm like some kind of jewel. She gleams and sparkles with priceless beauty.

I'm going to have an even harder time taking her home. I'm sure we'll kiss and make out in the limo again. I'll find it much harder to hold myself back and say goodbye to her at her apartment door.

I want her so freakin' bad I can't stand it. I want all of her right now—tonight. I don't want to wait any longer. I want to tear that dress off.

Just that one small taste of her breasts in my mouth—her skin quivering when I kissed down her neck—my hands around her ass pulling her into my hard spike....

Jesus, what the hell am I getting myself into? I need her. I need her real bad. Don't ask me how in God's name I'm supposed to even get through the rest of the evening standing next to her in a public ballroom without tearing that dress off.

Sitting next to her in the limo will be that much harder. We'll be alone there. I'll be able to feel her energy and see her staring up at me with those soft, soulful eyes that tell me so clearly how much she wants it.

The other club members distract me—but only slightly. The guys come up to greet me, shake my hand, and welcome me. Then attention turns to Jocelyn.

Dante holds out his hand to her and kisses her knuckles. "I almost didn't recognize you, Detective."

"Jocelyn isn't here in a professional capacity, Dante," I tell him. "She's here as my date."

Now his eyes widen when he looks down at her a second time. "My mistake. You'll both have to forgive me if I find it difficult to call you by your first name.....Jocelyn."

She blushes and smiles at him. Christ, she makes me weak in the knees when she blushes like that. "That was excellent, Dante. Now repeat it a hundred times and you'll be all set to go."

She makes him laugh, and like magic, a bunch of the women come over to greet her.

They introduce themselves to her one after the other and tell her who they're married to and what their business connections are. She talks to them back on that side while I get caught up in conversation with Dante, Lane, and Giovanni when they come over next.

I catch snatches of Jocelyn's conversations with Paige Novak espe-cially. Kevin has been telling Paige more than she ever wanted to know about Jocelyn's investigation—and then Demetrius himself comes over to confront her.

He does it in his usual suave way. He comes over to us guys first, exchanges a few pieces of small talk with me and the others, and then turns to Jocelyn.

He holds out his hand to shake hers. "It's a pleasure to see you again, Detective." He lets his gaze drag down her body. He doesn't shy away from checking her out and letting everyone see him do it.

I should get offended by that when he's leering at my date right in front of me. I should tell him where to step off, but he's obviously doing it to get a rise out of both of us—especially me for bringing her in the first place.

Bringing her to the gala so she could canvas the club membership and check out Demetrius in his native habitat as it were was a delib-erately provocative act. I did it so she could confront him in public. I wanted to provoke him.

Part of me wants to punish him for going into business with me under false pretenses.

I don't know why, but I suddenly get a powerful gut feeling that he *did* launder money through the Corner Pocket Pool Hall, that he was heavily involved in something highly illegal, and that he probably killed Pinkerton, too.

I can't explain any of this to myself because I have no evidence or reason to suspect him. Anyone could have used the Spiderware name—but anyone *wouldn't* have used the name.

That name means a lot to Demetrius. The company was his ticket out of the South Bronx—one of the worst neighborhoods in New York.

He was the one who named Spiderware. The name means more to him than it does to anyone else. It's his *nom de guerre*—his superhero identity. It's the most obvious name for him to use as a code for himself.

I hate him for compromising me like this. He tricked me into taking part in an illegal business deal—actually five of them. The deals themselves might not have been illegal. They may have been completely legitimate.

He isn't, though. He's got at least one foot on the other side of the line. I wouldn't have done business with him at all if I had known he was even remotely connected to that world.

He knew that, too. He knew I wouldn't do business with him if I had known. He lied to me about his involvement in the crime world. He tricked me into doing deals I wouldn't have otherwise. I hate him for that.

That's why I brought Jocelyn—apart from the fact that she's drop-dead gorgeous, impossibly sweet, and she's one of the deepest thinkers I've met in a long time. I trust her. I would have brought her even if she was a penniless waitress working in some southside diner.

She isn't, though. She's a homicide detective. I really hope she busts Demetrius. I hope she ruins him and sends him to prison for being an underhanded thug like so many others.

He doesn't belong in the club. He doesn't belong at this gala. He doesn't belong out there walking the streets as a free man—not if he could really do something like this.

I don't say any of that out loud. I barely articulate it to myself. It all flashes through my mind in a split second while he stands there leering at my date—my woman. She's mine. She's as much mine as she's going to be just as soon as I finish winning her heart.

I already have won it. No one has to spell it out for me. She's mine for the taking. I just have to treat her right. She already wants to give herself to me. I see that every time I get near her. She aches for me.

Thinking that tightens a fist in my guts. I want to take her home tonight, but I can wait on that, too. I can wait as long as it takes—because she's already mine.

It takes me a split second to make all of those connections. I don't have to stop him from looking at her. He can admire her all he wants. He can live with the reality that she's here with me—and she'll leave with me.

Everyone here can get it through their heads that Jocelyn and I are together. We're going to be together for a long, long time if I have anything to say about it.

"I would have let you question me a long time ago if I had known I would be looking at *this* while you did it," he tells her.

"It's nice of you to say so, Mr. Runyon," she murmurs in her sexiest, sultriest voice. "You're quite the man of mystery, aren't you?"

"Who—me?" His hand flies to his heart. "There's nothing mysterious about me. I'm an open book."

"Maybe you'd like to tell me how you came up with the idea for Spiderware. You grew up in the South Bronx, didn't you? Your mailing address was listed there until you turned eighteen. Then you moved to Manhattan and started the company. You attended South Bronx High School, but the school has no record that you graduated. I'm curious how a man of such humble beginnings developed such a sophisticated piece of software."

His features go hard. "I'm afraid that's proprietary information, Detective. I know you aren't familiar with corporate law, but I would be violating copyright by telling you that."

"I'm not asking you to share proprietary information," she breezes. "I'm asking how you developed it, when you developed it, and how you went from dodging gang battles in the Bronx to founding one of the most lucrative private contract businesses on the Eastern Seaboard. I'm sure the Pentagon and the Chinese Communist Party would also be interested to know."

He compresses his lips and then swallows in front of everyone. Gotcha.

I knew she had a few aces up her sleeve. She wouldn't be taking such a professional interest in Demetrius if she didn't have something on him. This has to be it. He might not even have developed Spiderware himself. Did he steal it from someone?

I become aware of a dozen people standing around listening to every damn word that comes out of her mouth. She could be single-handedly responsible for busting a crime lord who has been hiding out in our midst for the last year.

She answers all my questions for me. "Did you know Junior Osmond, Mr. Runyon?"

He pretends to raise his eyebrows again. "I've never heard that name before. Should I know him?"

"He went to South Bronx High School at the same time you did. You were in the same grade level and you even shared three classes with him—Math, Chemistry, and Computer Science. It turns out that Junior was a computer software prodigy. He developed a piece of software that reduced the amp friction load on the Tri-State power grid. He won the Article One Innovation Competition for his invention and the Federal Emergency Management Agency purchased the program from Junior while he was still at the competition celebrating his victory. Did you know that, Mr. Runyon? Is any of this ringing a bell at all?"

"No, I can't say I knew him," Demetrius replies. "I think I would remember that."

"Oh, I'm sure you would because he was murdered less than six months later. A group of unknown assailants ambushed him and stabbed him to death in an alley after school on his way home to his family apartment. The Police explained the killing as just another byproduct of all the crime in the area. They never found out who did it. His death was widely condemned and his loss mourned all over the school. You even got three days off from school in honor of his achievements. The principal held a special assembly to honor Junior after his death on the day before the three-day break. The principal and several teachers spoke at length about Junior being a software genius. Not even advanced adult programmers could keep up with him."

Dead silence answers her. Demetrius doesn't say a word in his own defense. He can't because he doesn't have one. The rotten cocksucker must have stolen Spiderware from the kid who developed it and then killed the guy to keep him quiet.

Now everyone in the club knows Demetrius is a fraud and a murderer. Who knows what the hell else he might be?

I can't wait to hear what meaningless nonsense he comes up with to try to deflect this, but a flurry of activity distracts everyone back toward the entrance doors.

Jackson and Mckenna come in followed by Derek and Vivian. I didn't notice until now that they weren't here yet.

Everyone takes the opportunity to talk about something else. Some other women who didn't hear the conversation between Jocelyn and Demetrius come over to greet me and ask me to introduce them to my date.

These women have no connection to Spiderware. Some of these women aren't even in business. They find Jocelyn's career fascinating and she finds theirs equally fascinating.

They all start talking about something different and the subject of Spiderware gets lost in the general hubbub. I wind up talking to other people, too, but Jocelyn and I stay near each other all evening. I don't want to let her out of my sight.

Chapter 22: Diego

I finish off the gala by talking to Paige and Kevin about our current deal. It always happens this way with everyone in the club at every event. We catch up on each other's lives and then the talk inevitably turns to business.

Paige gets called away to go do something or other and Kevin has to go greet some people who were invited to the gala as guests. That leaves me on my own.

Jocelyn is talking to Samantha Mulholland about some other NYPD detective Samantha knew at one point, but Jocelyn tells her that the guy is retired now.

They both go on at length about what a great guy he was and how he helped Lane and Samantha out of a tough spot.

That's the moment Demetrius chooses to come up on my other side. He must have been waiting for a break in the conversation so he could talk to me alone. He couldn't make it more obvious if he set up a billboard.

"I hope you don't think I'm involved in this money-laundering business, Diego," he tells me. "I don't know what this detective has been telling you about me, but I would never engage in anything like this."

"Jocelyn hasn't told me anything about the case, Demetrius. I've told everyone in the club the same thing. She's an extremely scrupulous cop. She plays her cards close to her vest and she doesn't let her personal feelings cloud her professional judgment."

"Still," he counters. "You should have realized she only asked you to bring her to the gala so she could question me—so she could question us. You must realize that."

I cock my head in mock interest. "What makes you think she asked me to bring her to the gala? What makes you think I didn't ask her?"

His eyes fall out of their sockets. "You did? Why would you do that?"

"I'm going out with her. Didn't you know? I've taken her on a handful of dates and then the gala came up. That's why I brought her. We have an agreement not to discuss her cases—ever since she helped me in the Montgomery Sinclair investigation. She told all of us during our first meeting that she had nothing on you and that it was as likely that someone else used the Spiderware name as a code in Romeano Pinkerton's ledgers. You know this. You were there. That's the last thing she's told me about this case. She said you weren't a suspect as yet. That's why I agreed to bring her into the club—because she assured us all that she wouldn't ask about the case."

He frowns for a second before he corrects his expression. "Oh, I see."

"And in case you really wanted to know, Demetrius, I am the one who initially asked her out. She has always behaved toward me with the strictest professionalism—right up until that point when I did ask her out. I'm quite certain she'll conduct herself with the same standard in this investigation. She's one of the most scrupulous individuals I've ever met. She would be the first person to stick up for you if she really thought you were innocent."

His expression clears the rest of the way. He didn't hear what I just said. She'll also be the first person to nail him to the wall if she gets the idea that he isn't innocent. She would be his best friend if he was. She would be his worst enemy if he wasn't.

My words actually make him start to smile. "That's very reassuring, Diego. I'm glad you see it that way. Thank you for telling me."

I don't clarify that she said that at the beginning of the investigation. She obviously doesn't see him the same way now—for obvious reasons.

"I never pegged you for the kind of guy who would date a cop," he remarks.

"Why do you say that? She's an outstanding, exceptional individual. She's smart, sensitive, trustworthy, beautiful..."

He bursts out laughing to interrupt me. "You can say that again."

I don't correct him on that, either. I don't want to talk to him about Jocelyn—or anything else. I definitely don't trust him now.

Like something out of my fondest dreams, she finishes her conversation just then and glides over to my side. She slips her arm through mine and stands extra close to me oozing sex appeal. She smiles up at Demetrius.

"Am I missing something here?" she purrs.

"Not at all. Demetrius here assumed that you asked me to bring you so you could question him about the Pinkerton case. I was just telling him that you and I are going out now. Oh, and I forgot to mention, Demetrius. I picked out Jocelyn's dress, shoes, and jewelry for tonight. What do you think? I'm delighted with the results. Aren't you?"

I give him a hard look, turn her away, and we sail off into the crowd. "What was that about?" she murmurs under her breath.

"Nothing you need to worry about. Demetrius is freaking out because he realizes you suspect him. He wanted to reassure me of his innocence."

"You didn't tell him that I asked you to bring me?"

"He assumed you asked me so you could question him and others about this investigation."

"But I did ask you so I could question him and others about this investigation."

I turn to face her in the middle of the ballroom. The rest of the world disintegrates. I'm alone with her here. "I would have asked you anyway, Jocelyn. I'm proud to be going out with you and I want to show you off to the world."

She turns pink again. God, I love it when she blushes like that! Her eyelashes dip. "You're really sweet."

"I'm proud of the way you talked to him before. This is exactly the kind of information we need." I slip my arm behind her back and lower my voice. "I really want to kiss you right now. I want to do even more than that."

"He's watching us," she half-whispers back. "He's watching us from across the room."

"Good. I hope they're all watching."

Her hand comes to rest on my jacket. Even that light touch sends a lightning bolt through me. I want her right this minute.

I want to ask her to marry me right now. I want to sweep her off her feet and carry her home to my bed, but I suppose I can't do that. I have to be a gentleman about this. I'm not a caveman.

I would like to be, though. I would like to be a caveman with her.

Thinking that starts to get me worked up again, so I pull her hand through my arm and steer her toward one of the waiters who is handing out champagne flutes. I take one for her, one for me, and touch my glass to hers.

"Here, here," I tell her.

She bursts into a grin. "What are we celebrating?"

"We're celebrating you in that outfit. We're celebrating me going out with you. We're celebrating me going public with the whole club about our relationship. That's something to celebrate, don't you think?"

She glances around. "You were right about these people. Some of them are really amazing. I feel inspired."

"What do you feel inspired to do? You're already doing it, aren't you?"

"Yes, I am. I don't know. It's like you were saying. These people inspire me to do more—to make more of a contribution."

"I don't see how you can make more of a contribution than you already are. Do you know how important a good Police officer is? You saved my life, Jocelyn. You know that. I'm sure you give people their lives back every day. You shouldn't sell yourself short on this career of yours. It's important—very important."

She beams at me. "Thank you. I really needed to hear that after standing in the same room with all these high-powered people."

"Do you remember what it was like when you worked at the diner?" I ask.

She frowns. "Yes, I remember. Why do you ask about that?"

"Do you remember when your fiancé mentioned going to the Police Academy and how you felt when you decided that you wanted to go, too?"

Her expression goes blank and she looks away and down at the floor. "Yeah," she mumbles. "I remember everything about how it happened."

"Do you remember what you thought your life would be like and how different it would be after you became a cop? You thought you would be a different person, that you would have so much more confidence, that you wouldn't be plagued by these constant doubts and self-hatred that you were *just* a waitress. You thought you would finally be happy because you were doing a job that mattered and getting paid good money for it. You thought you would actually be someone. You thought you would someone people admired, someone who could make a difference, someone people thought was smart and had their shit together. That's what you thought you would become by becoming a Police officer—and that's exactly what you did become. You're living the dream. You're the person you set out to become. You got all that confidence, the admiration, the purpose, the contribution—you got everything you dreamed of when you went to the Academy and became a cop. You have no reason to leave it to go looking for those things elsewhere. You're already doing it. Maybe that's why you don't see it—because you're in the middle of it. Everyone on the outside looking at you can see it. We can all see you making a difference and being a strong, confident, smart, savvy, connected individual."

She gazes up at me for a long minute. Then she touches her glass to mine. "Here, here."

"What are you toasting?" I ask.

"I'm toasting me going out with you. I'm toasting everyone in the world finding out that I'm with you. I'm proud to be with you and I'm proud of the fact that you're showing me off to the world. I hope I can do you justice."

"You do. You do it in spades. I couldn't ask for more than what you're already doing."

She takes one slow, blistering, suggestive step toward me, but she doesn't touch me. Her fingertips look so elegant holding her champagne glass.

"I really want to kiss you right now," she murmurs. "I want what we had in the limo."

"We will have that again, baby," I husk. "I swear it."

A wave of color sweeps over her face, down her neck, and vanishes under her dress. Her skin washes with energy and excitement at those words.

"You turn me on so much, baby," I whisper. "I can't get enough of you."

"I want you!" she croaks. "I need you so bad!"

"You have me, baby. You have me right here in front of you. I see you. I see how much you want it—and you're all mine. You're in my hands right now. You're mine to kiss and tease and touch. I'm going to enjoy you for a long, long time. Don't worry about that."

She gulps and her eyes zoom around the room in wild panic. She probably wants to leave so I can take her back to the limo. My God, she is so intoxicating!

I take her hand. "Come with me, baby," I murmur. "We aren't ready to leave just yet."

I lead her across the ballroom. People greet us and smile at us when they see me leading her by the hand. I want them to see that I'm with her.

I escort her through the crowds and we step out onto a balcony overlooking the street in front of the hotel. It's busy at this time of night. Light and noise flood the street. People walk up and down, talk, laugh, yell, and some try to sell each other things.

The darkness swallows me and Jocelyn out here. Heavy velvet drapes hang on either side of the balcony doors to give it some privacy.

I lead her to the railing where we can look over the side. It's cooler out here, so I take off my jacket and hang it around her shoulders.

She smiles up at me. "Thank you."

I ease over close to stand next to her. I didn't bring her out here so we could pretend we don't feel this way about each other.

The energy between us explodes the minute I get near her. I kiss her on the forehead, but my body is already going crazy just from holding her hand and gazing at her.

I let my hungry lips sink onto her neck and then ease the jacket aside so I can drag my mouth down her bare shoulder. I need to taste her. I need to inhale her.

She whimpers in deep agony and rests her head against mine as one tremor after another pulses through her. She gasps again and again trembling all over from the tension. I don't know how much more of this I can stand.

I let my arm snake behind her back and draw her closer to me—close enough to burn me with the stoppable power coming from both of us. I have to feel her. I have to experience her.

She leans against me so I feel her body aching for me. I never thought it could be like this with anyone—but it isn't just her body, her lips, and her beauty that captivates me. It's her pure, beautiful being—the person that she is.

I pull her in, but she still stands sideways from me. I don't try to turn her to face me. I stroke her body through this dress that mesmerizes me so much. She quivers and shivers all over when I touch her. She gasps out when I kiss the side and back of her neck.

I take a risk by moving behind her and wrapping my arms around her from behind. Her weight sinks against me and her head lies back on my shoulder. She touches my hands and arms when I stroke her delicious sides, arms, thighs, and hips.

I can't stop shaking from the energy between us. She electrifies me until I can't stand the tension. Something has to give. She straightens up, turns around to face me, and rests her arms around my neck. My hands disappear under my jacket around her magnificent body.

She gazes up at me all warm and buzzing with desire and emotion. She feels as overwrought and tremulous as I do.

I fall into her lips and tongue. Her fingers thread into my hair and she presses her breasts and body against my suit. She must feel how much I want her.

A clang interrupts us from inside the ballroom. I tear myself away from her and turn around to see what it is. The noise sounds like it's coming from the catering kitchen. A few different members head in that direction to see what's going on.

In that moment, I spot Demetrius leaving the gala early and alone. He takes advantage of everyone's distraction to slip away unnoticed.

"He's a snake," Jocelyn mutters.

I glance at her and see her watching him, too. I take her hand. "Let's get out of here. I don't think either of us is very good company right now—except to each other."

Chapter 23: Jocelyn

I slip back into Diego's limo and he gets in with me. The car heads off downtown to take me back to my apartment.

Diego turns in my direction—and his eyes inevitably migrate back to my dress. He doesn't act on it, though. He just glances at me and faces front.

He said we would do more of what we did on the way here. I don't want to push it if he isn't interested. I know he is interested. Maybe he thinks he has to hold back for my sake.

I don't say anything, either. I take his jacket off my shoulders and give it back to him. I don't need it anymore. The heater in the car makes it warm enough.

"Thank you for taking me to the gala," I tell him. "I really appreciate it."

"I'm sorry you didn't get more of a chance to question Demetrius. It wasn't a very fruitful evening, was it?"

"It was perfect. It was exactly what I needed."

His head shoots up. "It was? But he didn't tell you anything."

"He was never going to tell me anything. That wasn't the point."

"I don't understand." He frowns. "What was the point if not to get information out of him?"

"I did get information out of him—and I unsettled him in front of the club. That's what I wanted—to confront him and see how he responded. He acted guilty—don't you think? He sure looked guilty to me."

"Guilty of killing Junior Osmond, maybe. You didn't ask him anything about Pinkerton or the money-laundering."

"If he was capable of killing Junior, he's capable of killing Pinkerton. The point is that he has something to hide—which makes him a suspect. I wasn't sure, but I am now. That on its own makes the evening a success."

He grins at me. "It wasn't a success because you sat on my lap and let me undress you?"

My smile vanishes. Those words....the memory of sitting on his lap.....

He turns me on more than any man I've ever known. Standing or sitting near him feels like some kind of drug.

I lace my fingers into his to hold his hand and lean in to kiss him. I want to do more than that, but I feel it just from sitting next to him, holding hands, and kissing.

He responds instantly, straps his arm around my waist, and lifts me back onto his lap in the same position while we kiss. He pushes my dress up so I straddle him with my thighs exposed. He can see my panties underneath, but just barely.

He plunges one hand between my legs and rubs me in circles there to spiral me out of my mind. I need him so bad and my thoughts make it true.

He rips off my mouth, dives into my chest, and nibbles my nipples through my dress. He uses his mouth to pull it down, pushes my bra aside, and his mouth closes around me in hot, inevitable madness.

I yelp as the passion between us erupts past the breaking point and he glides his fingers into my dripping channel. He's been making me fantasize about this all evening just by standing near him.

He works me back and forth on his hand while he devours my breasts in rooting, animal madness. I can feel how hard he is, but he doesn't try to take it out or do it with me more than this.

I slam down on his hand and spike into outer space on a blasting orgasm that splits me apart. I scream and thrust down harder, but he's already pulling me toward him in an unstoppable rhythm.

I throw back my head and convulse in his iron grip. He clamps his arm around me harder so he doesn't lose his hold on me. I need more....and more....I need it all.

I collapse sobbing on his shoulder as the convulsions peak out of all control. It's happening. I'm losing control with him.

He starts to lose control with me, too—except that he never loses control. He seizes me even before I finish thrashing in his arms, picks me up, and turns me backward to straddle him facing the other way.

I don't even know what's happening to me. Everything he does is so blisteringly hot and erotic that I can't think straight.

He peels my dress down, yanks my bra the rest of the way off so my breasts hang free in the night air, and takes hold of one of my arms by the elbow. He plants one hand behind my neck and pushes me so I bend over with my ass pointed backward toward him.

This position turns me on beyond anything I can imagine—and then he crams his hand between my legs from behind.

He pulls me back onto his fingers and bumps his hand deep and hard into me while he uses my arm to pull me back into those strokes. I fold forward and my breasts swing out in such a hot, sensual, delicious rhythm.

I moan and gyrate on his hand climaxing again and again. I might as well be doing it with him right here in his limo. I really wish I was. I need that more than anything.

I'm still fogged out of my brain on so many aphrodisiac endorphins and a cocktail of pleasure and excruciating satisfaction—but I'm not satisfied. Will anything or anyone ever satisfy me again?

The limo pulls to a halt in front of my building. Diego doesn't stop until I start to cycle down on my own.

He eases off the rhythm and lets me spiral my hips on his lap a few more times before he pulls me off.

He lays me on the seat sobbing, whimpering, and moaning in deepest, aching bliss. I can't even focus my eyes.

He pulls my dress down and straightens it over my legs like that's supposed to help me somehow. He keeps caressing me through the slippery, sexy, satin fabric.

I finally pull it together enough to tug my bra back into place and draw my dress straps up over my shoulders. I can't stop wincing and grimacing as the last shuddering tremors fade out and dissipate to my fingers and toes.

I need to crawl into bed and disappear from the world while I try to wrap my head around everything that happened tonight—and I don't mean between me and Demetrius Runyon.

This thing between me and Diego—I don't understand it. I don't understand how a man can affect me this much. I feel so much for him. His very presence rewrites the rules of reality into something I never thought possible.

I need so much more of it, but I don't know how to tell him that. He knows I like him. He might even know that I need him. I just don't think he knows how much I need him.

He waits for me for a long time. He keeps stroking my body, my face, my arms, my hair, and my back until I put myself together enough to sit up.

His eyes speak volumes. He looks heartbroken, pleased, and concerned all at the same time. He bores into my soul through our eyes until I can't handle looking at him anymore. I glance out the window.

He takes that signal, get out of the car, and takes my hand to help me out. He puts my hand through his arm and escorts me inside to the elevator.

I can't bear the thought of riding up to my apartment in silence. I need something from him—something important. I can't face tonight after he leaves—not without something.

I rest my head on his shoulder and my eyes sink shut. He lets his head fall against mine, kisses my hair, and then turns around to put his arms around me.

My head collapses onto his chest and I shut my eyes in the warm halo of his protection. He grips the back of my neck, pulls my head against his heart, and presses his mouth against my scalp while the elevator climbs the rest of the way to my floor.

I'm still standing there in a sex-drunk fog when the elevator stops and the doors open. I should stand up straight and function like an adult, but Diego doesn't let me.

He holds me in that position against his chest, walks backward a few steps to leave the elevator, and stops there to keep holding me.

I can't cope. I just stand here with my eyes closed. I don't know what to do next or how to snap out of this hazy place between what we did in the limo and getting back to normal life.

Diego shifts his head slightly and murmurs into my fevered brain. "Take me into your apartment, baby."

I can't think. I open my eyes just enough to walk off down the corridor to my apartment. Thank God he still keeps my hand inside the bend of his elbow. He's always there to steady me. I couldn't do anything without his help.

He stops by the apartment door and waits while I take my keys out of my purse and unlock the door.

I'm embarrassed that a billionaire is seeing me living in such a shitty apartment. I can just imagine what his house looks like. It's probably some kind of mansion or something.

He barely notices the apartment. He waits just long enough for me to push the door open and turn on a single floor lamp in the living room. Then he takes over, shuts the door behind him, throws the deadbolt, and leads me over to the couch.

He sits down first and eases me down to sit sideways on his lap. I collapse into his arms. I can't function anymore and now I don't have to because he's here.

He guides my head down onto his shoulder and settles back on the quilt cradling me in such a tender embrace. I can't help but moan in perfect relief. He's here. He's taking care of me. He's everything I need right now.

I shut my eyes and let myself drift off. I barely notice him stroking my legs through my dress, up to my hips, my sides, my arms, and my hair. His hands feel good and comforting and protective enough for me to drift off.

He demands nothing of me except that I lean on him and let him hold me. That's exactly what I need right now.

Chapter 24: Jocelyn

I wake up in darkness when Diego stands up from the couch, lifts me in his arms, and carries me into the bedroom. Don't ask me how he knows where it is except that he could probably see that from his position on the couch.

The neon sign on the building roof next door casts a ghostly reddish glow into the bedroom. It gives Diego enough light to see where he's going. He lays me down on the bed, sinks onto his knees on the mattress, and stretches out next to me.

I'm still half-asleep when my eyes drift up to meet his. He props himself on his elbow gazing down at me. His hands keep making the same migration over my body. I barely have the brain power to register that he's lying on my bed in my bedroom.

He doesn't pay attention or even seem to notice the room. He never takes his eyes off me. A slight smile curls up the corners of his lips and he lets his eyes slide down to my body. He watches his hands touching me all over.

That appreciative look makes me want him again. I lift my arms to put them around his neck. I want to kiss him and pull him down on top of me, but he doesn't give me a chance.

He looks up at me with a very different gleam in his eye. My body automatically stiffens at that look. His touch changes even though he doesn't grope me or do anything else to me. He squeezes my outer thigh and then my hip. He crumples my dress under his grip.

He holds eye contact and moves extra slowly so I can see everything he's doing. He lays his hand on my arm, slithers it up to my wrist, and pulls my arm away from his neck. He pushes my arm above my head and then does the same thing with my other arm.

He extends both of my arms above my head so my body lies extended and arched in front of him. He goes back to running his hand all over me and caressing me through my dress, but now that touch charges my skin with blistering energy.

He strokes up my sides and around the sides of my breasts without actually touching them. He even strokes between them and over my bare chest, but he doesn't touch my breasts themselves or make any move to take my dress off—not yet.

His touch and the commanding look in his eyes holds me captive no matter what. I can't move except to tremble under his hand, stare into his hypnotic eyes, and feel his power.

This position excites me to new heights. I want him to touch me. I want to feel him handle my breasts and touch me between my legs.

We're going there tonight. His eyes tell me that loud and clear. Tonight is the night. We're going to do it, but only when he's ready to.

He eventually gets around to pulling my arms down, slipping my dress straps off my shoulders, and sliding my whole dress down my body, over my stomach, down my thighs, and I kick it off along with my shoes.

I lie in front of him in my bra and panties, but that doesn't satisfy him. He rolls me away from him, unhooks my bra, and takes it off as he rolls me into my old place on my back.

He sits up, hooks my panties, and draws them off before he returns to propping himself on his elbow. He pushes my arms back above my head so he can see my whole body laid out for him.

That's what this is. I'm his now. He knows it when he looks at my body. He just has to decide how to enjoy it, now that I'm finally giving myself to him.

He teases every inch of me with his maddening fingertips. He doesn't shy away from touching my breasts, circling my nipples, and dragging his fingers up my inner thighs, grazing my swollen tissues, and continuing over my belly to make me shudder.

I can't stop staring at him even though he isn't watching me. He observes his own hands stimulating me, delivering slight pinches to my nipples to make me moan, and rolling me onto my back so he can find all the most sensitive places there, too.

He pushes me down on my stomach, rolls toward me, and starts dragging his hot mouth and tongue up, down, and all over my back. I shiver when he hits certain sensitive spots and then I scream when he bites down on my ass.

I rear off the bed, but he holds me down and mouths farther down to my thighs. He buries his face between my legs and starts crawling his scorching, open-mouthed kisses up my inner thighs getting closer to my slit.

I try to spread my legs to let him in, but he holds me in position by lying on top of me from behind. He gets as far as the crease of my ass before he decides to sit up, roll me back onto my back, and lie down next to me again.

I can't stop moaning and jolting from all the mind-blowing energy he's giving me. I want to touch him, but he pushes my arms up so he can go back to teasing me. His touch gets more insistent, more demanding, more possessive.

The smile on his face turns predatory. He's going to lose control with me, but he isn't there yet. I whine in his face praying to God Almighty he sees how much I need him.

He goes back to dangling his fingertips all over me, but things change when he makes his way back down to my thighs.

He crushes them in a tight grip and makes me gasp. Here it comes. He squeezes up my thighs to my mound and starts circling my clitoris in soft, gentle, feather-light strokes. I need so much more than this. I need all of him the way he did it in the car.

He takes mercy on me by leaning in and kissing me. His kiss explodes me apart. I can't hold back. I howl into his mouth as his teasing circles get harder and stronger. He escalates just as fast and plows his fingers back inside me.

I hurl myself at him so much harder this time. I need this. I need to climax—and I do. I scream and buck against his hand. Will he ever take me? Will he ever let me touch him in return and make tonight as comforting and complete as I need it to be?

He reduces me to a quivering mass of nerves lying on the bed. I'm still howling and sobbing in the throes of so much climax when he sits all the way up, pivots onto his knees, and starts stripping his clothes off fast and furious.

The red light coming from outside casts alluring shadows between the muscles of his lean, chiseled torso. His chest strains when he puts his arms behind him to take them out of his sleeves.

His back spreads out in a fan of muscle when he sits down on the bed to untie his shoes, kick them off, and then to slide his pants down.

He pauses just for an instant to put his phone on the bedside table before he throws his clothes on the floor. He pulls down the covers, starts crawling underneath them, and holds them up so I can do the same thing.

I burrow into bed and wrap myself around his naked body in matchless, soul-crushing relief. His warmth and strength envelop me in bliss—and desire. Our skin fuses in a river of heat and velvet, comforting hunger. I can't get enough of him.

He leans over to kiss me, pulls me on top of him, and steers my thighs apart to straddle him. His hard shaft touches my sensitive, twitching flesh and my wetness coats it. I crave him.

His eyes smolder up at me from below. That look commands me to give myself to him in every possible way. My body and soul ache for him.

I rock on his hardness and feel his length plowing my puffy, swollen petals apart. He exhales a deep, guttural breath when he feels me stimulating myself to ride down on him.

His hands close on my ass from behind, but he doesn't adjust my pace. He lets me take my time while we kiss to the ends of the earth.

I push myself up on my arms so I can look down at him. He gazes up at me, but this position convinces me more than anything else ever could that he's the one possessing me. It could never be any other way.

His eyes hold me in their old unbreakable grip. He watches me sway and angle myself to stroke on his shaft. I tease myself to the limit and work him closer and closer to the point of no return.

He caresses my breasts as they undulate in his face. He follows my hips in their inevitable spiral to the moment we're both waiting for.

Without warning, he rears off the bed, grabs hold of my breasts, and steers them into his mouth. He stays half sitting up just long enough for me to ride down on him and his long, stiff, solid meat impales me to the core.

I scream, but he isn't finished yet. He said we would do again what we did in the limo and now he does it. He waits just long enough for me to straddle him before he blasts off the bed, sits all the way up with me riding him to kingdom come, and he seizes me to take over.

He pulls me down on him while he devours my breasts in ravaging mouthfuls. He sits all the way up on the bed and then pivots onto his knees so he can drive up into me from below.

His thickness blasts my mind apart. I never thought it would be like this. His constant attention and stimulation leave me sensitive and ready for him. I start to climax as soon as he thrusts into me.

He bangs me upward again and again. I peak on every thrust and fly into a frenzy of struggling and thrashing against his arms. I don't want to break out of it. I need him to hold me together before I fly apart into a million pieces.

He seems to understand that I need this. I need to fly completely out of control and for him to contain me inside his own ferocity.

He growls at me while he sucks and teases my nipples to madness. I can't survive the explosive tidal wave of ecstasy and stimulation consuming me in madness.

He clamps his muscular arms around me and thumps in deep, hard, shattering strokes that detonate my world apart. I plant my hands on his shoulders trying to fight my way out of this insanity.

I want him to hurl me down on his rod again and again without stopping. He's already doing it, but I go completely off the deep end. The thought of him stopping destroys my last shred of reserve.

He's holding me in his bare arms, crushing me against his naked body, and plowing into me hard and fast enough to make me writhe and convulse in one volatile wave of destruction after another.

I keep spiking into another climax every time he slams into me. I barely have time to drift down when he pulls out before he drives in for another one. I'm too out of my mind even to realize what's happening to me.

I'm still screaming my head off with so many orgasms when he topples forward, lays me on my back on the bed, and stretches out on top of me between my spread thighs. Now he's the one who props himself on his arms so he can stare down at me from above.

He steers my arms above my head. He likes seeing me like this. I arch into his thrusts and feel his thick, veiny, rigid shaft gliding into and out of me on a blissful, shimmering galaxy of sparks.

They ripple up my channel each time he spirals into me. Then he makes me scream with bliss when he pulls out. My body shivers and quakes underneath him.

I have trouble maintaining eye contact with him. I wind up clamping my eyes shut when he drives me to another climax. Then I stare into the dark pools of his soul when he draws out and brings a gush of hot nectar from my channel.

I'm floating in such a deep chasm of space that I can't think of anything other than how much I feel for him right now. He gives me so much pleasure, but he always takes care of me. He held me on the couch for hours before he brought me to bed.

I cherish every minute I spend with him. This is just the latest in a long series of tendernesses between us. This is the latest in him giving me exactly what I need in the right way at the right time.

He lets his rhythm cycle down and eventually pivots sideways to lie down on his side on the bed with my legs still wrapped around his waist. He slows even more, pulses inside me very slowly for a long, long time, and gazes deep into my eyes while we kiss.

He eventually slows down enough that he pulls out and stops. I don't know why. I've never had sex with a guy who stopped without finishing himself off.

I don't even know how many orgasms he's given me tonight, but he doesn't seem too interested in having even one of his own.

He doesn't break eye contact. He lies there kissing me and stroking my body in long, easy, comforting caresses until I power the rest of the way down.

He still has his eyes open studying me to the depths of my soul by the time I crash into a black, dreamless slumber.

Chapter 25:
Diego

I watch the light change in Jocelyn's bedroom as the sun creeps over the building roofs outside her window. The sunlight eventually drowns out the red neon glow coming from the sign on the roof next door.

I must have worn her out because she sleeps for a long time. I'm not tired enough to sleep. Doing it with her gives me more energy than I know what to do with. I could go out and run a marathon right now, but watching her sleep is more interesting.

She's absolutely exquisite when she gives herself to me—exactly the way I knew she would be. She lets go completely and releases herself to go as far as I want to take her. No woman has ever done that with me before.

I have to control myself not to keep taking her again and again—possibly forever. I had to force myself to power down. She's too precious and she wears herself out too fast by climaxing so much.

I can wait. I get just as much stimulation out of watching her and enjoying her as I would from finishing myself off. I care about her too much to just use her for my own momentary satisfaction. I can get that anytime.

Taking care of her feels so much better. I love how much she puts herself in my hands. Is it possible that she trusts me as much as I trust her? I know she does. She shows a dimension of vulnerability to me that she doesn't show the outside world.

What idiots these guys are not to accept her as they find her. They run out on her when they find out what she does for a living. How stupid is that?

Those moments of unguarded vulnerability mean more because she's so confident, self-possessed, and competent in her daily life. She can be a superhero out there. She's soft, sensitive, and fragile in here with me.

Her trust makes me feel a thousand times stronger and more confident. She's safe with me now and she always will be. I will never violate her vulnerability. That's my pledge. I earn her trust and I'll damn well keep it.

She sleeps for a long time, but I love that, too. I love that I can lie here and guard her. I'm the one who sees her asleep. I'm the one who makes sure nothing disturbs the rest she needs. Not even I disturb the rest she needs.

She starts to stir at nine o'clock the next morning. I've taken the time to answer work emails and straighten a few things out in the meantime. I can take as long as she needs me to. I'm not going anywhere.

She twists on the mattress a few times and her hair falls over her eyes. I rake it out of her face and kiss her on the forehead. "Good morning, beautiful angel," I murmur.

She groans, buries her face in the pillow, and starts to drift off again before she jolts wide awake. She shoots up, props herself on her elbow, squints around the bedroom, and collapses back on the mattress covering her eyes. "Oh, no!" she growls.

"What's wrong?"

"Don't look at anything in this crappy apartment, okay? Just don't look at anything."

"What's wrong with it?" I wind up looking around much more closely than I did before. "It looks like a normal apartment to me. Do you have closets full of hoarded clutter? Something tells me you don't."

"It's just dumpy." She rolls onto her side all glowing and naked and peeks out at me from under her hair. "I hate to think what your house looks like."

"I didn't always live in the house I live in now. I grew up in an apartment almost identical to this one."

Her head shoots up and her eyes pop. "You did?"

"It had three bedrooms—one for my parents, one for my brothers and me, and one for my sister. How many does this one have?"

"Um....two." She frowns at me. "Are you serious? Your father was a diplomat."

"Being a diplomat in Spain doesn't mean you earn a giant salary. We were hardly even middle class. Madrid was expensive in those days. The apartment was all he could afford, but it was very comfortable." I look around again. "Yes, it was almost exactly like this one except the kitchen and living room was a different kind of layout. We didn't have that counter between them. We had the family dinner table there."

She sinks back on the pillows. "I had no idea. I don't know why I thought you grew up better off than that." She raises her eyebrows and shrugs. "I guess I'll put that on the list of all the other preconceived ideas I had about you."

"What about you? You said your family was in Brooklyn. Is that where you're from?"

She winces and looks away. "No, I'm not from there."

I wait for her to say something else. "Where are you from, then?"

She rolls onto her back and stares at the ceiling. "I lived in a tiny, no-name farming village in the mountains of central Vietnam until I was ten. That's when my parents moved here with me, my brother, and my sister. My brother was eleven and my sister was four. She doesn't remember the move, but I do. I didn't want to come. I was happy there in our own village. I knew everyone and they all knew me. Half the people in the village were my relatives. They all helped each other farm and we saw each other all the time. It was a beautiful life and the only one I'd ever known. Then my parents moved to Brooklyn and they both had to take jobs working long hours. I absolutely hated it here. I hated everything about it. I hated the city. I hated the people. I hated the language. I hated the customs. I hated living in a separate apartment away from other people. I spent the next ten years dreaming about earning enough money to leave and go back to Vietnam, but by then it was too late. I guess that's one of the reasons I got the job at the diner. I didn't do well in school because I was in protest of the whole thing. I learned to speak English and I made sure to do it so I wouldn't have an accent. That's all I did so I wouldn't get picked on at school. I protested everything else and deliberately did badly in school so I wouldn't succeed. It all seems so stupid now."

"Is that what happened with your first boyfriend? Was he Vietnamese, too? Is that why he didn't want you to become a cop?"

"No, he was white. Sometimes I think he had the idea that he'd gotten himself a submissive mail-order bride from China or something and that's what set him up to expect me to act like his servant and personal doormat."

I remember something else. "How did you get the name Hitchcock if your parents are both Vietnamese?"

"They changed their name when they moved here. They named themselves after Alfred Hitchcock for some bizarre reason. That was another thing I hated. I hated the name. I spent all of those ten years secretly whispering my original name to myself under the covers in my bed at night to remind myself that I wasn't Jocelyn Hitchcock at all. I repeated the names of the towns nearest my home village and the names of all my relatives. It turned into a kind of litany to the past to keep it alive until I could go back there. It's stupid, I know. Most of my older relatives are all probably long dead by now."

"It isn't stupid at all. It helps me understand you." I kiss her. "It's a beautiful story. Would you like it if I called you by that name?"

She turns bright red and buries her face in the pillow laughing. "No! I wouldn't like it. I like it when you call me Jocelyn. I don't use my original name anymore. I let go of all of that when I joined the Academy. Jocelyn Hitchcock became my Police superhero name. It became the name of all the confidence and power I had been giving away to the past for all those years. It became the name of my new life—the best version of myself that I wanted my life to be."

"That's so beautiful," I exclaim. "I love that."

"I was really messed up about it for a long time, but the Academy and the Police Force gave me my life back." She stretches her arms above her head. "Now I'm all brand new." She laughs at the joke.

I can't help but kiss her. "What a wonderful story. You really are a superhero, aren't you?"

She laughs again and scoots in close to me. "I try. So what are we doing today?"

"What are *you* doing today? Are we staying in bed today to finish off the rest of your nervous system that I didn't completely demolish last night?"

She snickers and blushes at me. "Was it that obvious?"

"Um....yes. Maybe we should curtail our activities...."

"You better not! Don't even use the word, 'curtail' in the same sentence with that."

"With what?"

She shoves my shoulder. "Stop making fun of me. It isn't my fault you're a god in bed."

I snort. "I'm nothing of the sort. You were much more divine than I was."

She blushes and slithers all the way up to me and undulates her body all over me. "What about you? Are we going to spend the day completely demolishing your nervous system?"

"How would you do that?"

She burrows her arm under the covers and her hand closes around my package. I'm soft at the moment, but she changes that in a matter of seconds just by touching me. I start to get hard in her hand and she wraps her fingers around me.

"I bet I could find a way," she murmurs and nuzzles her face into my neck.

I'm certain she could find a way when she kisses me and strokes me like this. Taking charge and doing it to her produces a different effect on my body and mind than this does. Her touch somehow shatters me in ways nothing else does.

She starts inching down the bed leaving molten kisses on my chest and working her way down my stomach. I realize a second too late before her mouth closes on me.

I pull her off with an almighty effort. "No, baby," I choke. "Not that."

"I want to." She buries her head under the blankets and tries to get me in her mouth again. She wraps her tongue around me one more time before I stop her. "No." It takes all my willpower to say that one word. "No."

She looks up at me with her face still level with my throbbing shaft. "Why? Why don't you want me to?"

"It's degrading to you."

"No, it isn't. Would you use your mouth on me?"

"Of course. I would do it in a heartbeat to give you pleasure."

"Then I would want to do the same thing to give you pleasure. Isn't that what we both want?"

I turn my head away fighting back turmoil. "No, baby. Not that."

She gives it up, crawls up me, and drapes her body on top of me. Her naked flesh, stomach, and breasts lull me into a delicious ebb of pure ecstasy.

She kisses me for a while and then gets up on her hands and knees above me to steer me between her thighs. She doesn't ask again if she can pleasure me with her mouth.

She stays there on her hands and knees pumping me into her juicy channel. I can't get over how hot, wet, spongy, and responsive she is. She feels magical and heavenly.

She smiles down at me with a very different expression than I saw from her last night. She doesn't shatter. She wants to make me shatter.

Thinking that sets off my instincts. I sit up and carry her with me when I rotate onto my knees and push her down on the bed on her stomach.

I could think of a lot of ways I wanted to take her last night, but it was our first time. Now she wants to shatter me, so I'll just have to shatter her first. That shouldn't be too hard. I know exactly the right spots to tease.

I flip her onto her stomach and hold her down while I bury my face between her thighs from behind. She loved it when I did this last night, but I didn't take it as far as I wanted to.

She arches into me and tries to shove her ass in my face. She wants it as badly as I want to give it to her. I work up her thighs and deliver a few brutal licks to her dripping tissues from behind.

She blasts off the mattress from the spike in intensity. She would get away from me completely if I didn't hold her down.

I wait until she tries to arch into me one more time. Then I pivot onto my back and scoot my head between her legs. Gravity eventually pulls her down right into my mouth. I inhale her and consume her the way I wanted to before. She's on fire.

She screams when her weight puts pressure on her sensitive petals. I don't give her a single instant of rest before I plunge my fingers into her with one hand and pull her down on my face with the other.

We both have today off. We won't be going anywhere for a while. She is going to need a lot more sleep when I finish with her.

Chapter 26: Diego

I stroll into The Billionaires' Club and instantly sense something wrong. Everyone talks in hushed murmurs. No one laughs or raises their voices. I don't see anyone relaxing, eating, watching TV, or working on their phones or devices.

"What's going on?" I ask Kevin the minute I walk in.

"Haven't you heard? The DA is bringing charges against Demetrius Runyon for the murder of Romeano Pinkerton. Demetrius got arrested this morning. He's going in for an indictment hearing later today."

I can only nod. "I'm not surprised."

"You knew about this?!" Kevin gasps and then narrows his eyes at me. "Did you have something to do with this? Did Jocelyn cook up this case to pin it on Demetrius the same way the department pinned Montgomery's death on you?"

I have to fight my temper under control. "Jocelyn didn't cook up anything. For one thing, she isn't even responsible for making the decision to charge and indict someone for a crime. That decision comes from the DA."

"But she was the one who conducted the investigation." A few more people gather around. "She would have been the one who brought the evidence to the DA to make that decision."

"That's exactly my point. The DA wouldn't bring the case without evidence—compelling evidence." I find myself looking around at all the other members. "Jocelyn had no interest in Demetrius as a suspect when the Police started this investigation. She was as interested in proving that someone else was using the Spiderware name instead of Demetrius. She wouldn't have brought the case at all if she didn't have compelling evidence of his guilt."

"What evidence would that be?" Derek asks.

"I don't know. Where did you hear that the city was indicting him?"

Lane shows me a news story on his phone. I read the story as quickly as possible and gasp when I get halfway down the page. "The DA is charging him with Junior Osmond's murder, too."

Like something out of a bad dream, two other detectives show up just then. Dante brings them in this time.

"Diego Espinosa?" one of the detectives asks.

"Yes?" I ask. "Can I help you?"

The guy hands me a bunch of folded papers stapled together. "The DA is calling you as a witness in the case against Demetrius Runyon. The District Attorney's office would like you to make yourself available to testify on the date marked on those papers."

"I don't have any information to offer in the case against Demetrius Runyon. I wasn't involved in Romeano Pinkerton's operation and I didn't go to high school with Demetrius and Junior." I frown at them. "Why isn't Detective Hitchcock working on this case?"

"The case has already been handed over to the DA. All the detectives who were assigned to the Pinkerton murder investigation have been reassigned to other cases. We're only here to give you the paperwork. Just read it. The DA isn't calling you about either the Pinkerton murder or the Osmond murder. She's calling you to testify about your business dealings with Runyon—your dealings that had to do with how much involvement he usually took in fulfillment of his business contracts. Did he involve himself with rolling out the software or did he have teams of technicians do it all? That kind of thing."

I stare at the papers in my hand. I have to testify against another member of The Billionaires' Club. The club exists so we can defend and support each other—not testify against each other in murder cases.

I have to find out how far his criminality really ran. He might have transferred laundered money to me during our contractual transactions. I have to find out one way or the other—and I have to get him off the street and out of the club if he did do that.

The detectives go around the room delivering notices to Kevin, Paige, and a few other people who had dealings with Demetrius. The detectives call all these people to testify against him.

The two detectives eventually leave and a rush of rapid talk breaks out in the club. A bunch of guys get on their phones and laptops looking up any details of the case that have already been leaked to the press.

"We know more about the Junior Osmond murder than anyone in the press does," Niko points out. "Jocelyn told us more than we needed to know the night of the gala."

"It's pretty amazing she hunted into this as far back as Demetrius's high school days," Giovanni adds. "That's what I call dedication to the facts."

"She must have realized this couldn't be the first time he had killed someone. Listen to this." Jackson holds up his phone. "This story says the killer ambushed Pinkerton in the small hours of the morning, killed him with a through-and-through shot to the head near a brick wall where the bullet wouldn't lodge in the surface behind him, and then removed both the used bullet and the shell casing to eliminate as much evidence as possible. Someone that thorough couldn't have been doing it for the first time."

"That's interesting," Dante remarks. "The Police never found any evidence at the Junior Osmond crime scene, either."

I can't listen to any more of this. I have to see Jocelyn. I call her, but she has her phone turned off, so I text her to call me when she's available. She doesn't call until six o'clock. "Can I see you tonight?" I ask. "I really want to see you."

"Is this about you being called to testify against Demetrius?" she asks. "That was the DA's decision, not mine. This is only the indictment hearing. All you have to do is answer questions about your business dealings with him. You aren't under suspicion for anything—and we tracked all the money from your deals with him. None of it is involved in the money-laundering operation."

"I only want to see you partially about that. Just see me—please. When do you get off work?"

"I should be done in about an hour. Why don't you pick me up outside the station at seven?"

"I'll be there."

I get in my limo and ride downtown to the Police station. I get there first. She's five minutes late coming out of the building. "Sorry. I had to talk to the sergeant and clear up a few things."

"Never mind," I tell her. "What's going on with the Pinkerton murder?"

"You know as much as I do. The DA is handling it now. It's no longer with the Police Department. What happens from now on is out of my hands except that I have to testify against Demetrius, too.

I have to report on some of the information that came up in my investigation."

"It's Friday. Go out with me tonight."

Her head shoots up. "Is that why you came to see me—to ask me out? You could have done that over the phone."

"I mean go out with me tonight and spend the weekend with me at my place. I want you there. I don't want to keep going out like this and leaving the next morning or whenever."

She blinks at me. "I don't know if I'm ready to go to your place."

"It's just a house like any other."

"I'm sure it isn't like any other."

"Then just try it. If you absolutely hate it, we'll go back to staying at yours."

"You would actually stay...at my place?"

"I told you it's comfortable for me. I'm there to see you. I don't give a damn about your apartment. I just think you might be equally comfortable at mine. You might even decide to stay there and not go back to your apartment at all."

She gapes at me with her mouth open. "Are you seriously suggesting what I think you're suggesting?"

"Why not? Did you think I was doing this so I could make you my girlfriend? I wouldn't insult you with that."

"If I'm not your girlfriend....." She holds up her hand and shuts her eyes. "Don't answer that."

"Just come over and spend the weekend with me. Withhold judgment at least until you spend the weekend there. You don't have a problem spending the weekend with me elsewhere, do you? You don't have a problem going out with me in general. Am I right?"

"Of course not."

"Then a house is just a house and the people in it are what matters. Come with me. We'll stop by your place and you can pack whatever you need for the weekend. Then we'll go out to dinner and I'll take you home with me. Heaven knows you've taken me home with you enough times. I don't want to do that anymore."

She looks away. "All right. I guess I can't argue with that."

Chapter 27: Diego

J ocelyn and I get out of my limo. I go upstairs to her apartment with her while she puts a few things in a small leather carry bag. She refuses to look at me on our way out of the building.

"Don't be so nervous," I tell her. "We're going to dinner first and no one will make you go anywhere you don't want to go. If you can't stand the house, we'll go somewhere else. We can get a different one or a smaller apartment—whatever you want. I just want you with me. That's all."

She shoots me a terrified glance. "I'm really starting to wish I actually had moved back to Vietnam."

"Then you wouldn't be around to save all these people—including me. I wouldn't want that. It isn't just that I want you for myself. You wouldn't be happy going back to Vietnam now anyway. You're outgrown it."

"I know," she murmurs. "I'm just not ready to move into some billionaire's mansion."

"You wouldn't be moving into some billionaire's mansion. You would be moving in with me. I don't care where it is. We can get a room at the YMCA if you want us to."

She laughs for the first time. "And cook in an electric teakettle?"

"Yes, exactly. That sounds perfect as long as we're there together and we can sleep in the same bed every night. I don't care about anything else."

She slips her arm around me and kisses me on the cheek. "You're the sweetest guy I've ever met. Do you know that?"

"It's only because it's you. I wouldn't live at the YMCA with any of the guys from the club. I can promise you that."

She laughs again and we get back into the car. The driver puts her bag in the trunk so we can forget all about that.

He drives us all the way to the southern coast of Long Island, pulls into a long, wooded driveway, and drops us off in front of a prestigious resort overlooking the water.

"What is this place?" Jocelyn whispers on our way into the lobby.

"I decided you needed to take a vacation after the Pinkerton case wrapped. We're here to have some dinner, spend the night, and we can go home in the morning."

She beams at me while we wait our turn to check in at the front desk. "Thank you. I did need a vacation."

"Of course you did. You work way too hard."

She flushes and bursts into one of her grins. "Look who's talking."

We step up to the desk, check in, and I get the key. I take her hand and lead her to the resort's five-star restaurant. "Now I feel under-dressed," she murmurs.

"You look fine. You look like the superhero you are."

She blushes again, but the host takes us to our table just then so she can't contradict me. I take her hand across the table. "It will always just be you and me. It doesn't matter where we stay or what you wear. I want you and you want me. That's all there is to the decision."

Her full, delightful smile breaks across her face. "Yeah. That's what I want, too."

"Let's talk about the future," I tell her.

"*The* future?" she asks. "Or *our* future?"

"What's the difference? I want to move ahead with our relationship. I don't want to date anymore."

"So what's your question for me?"

"What do you see as the next step? I mean what do you want the next step to be? What would be the most comfortable step for you—after we've dated enough to know we want to take the next step?"

She shrugs and looks away. "I suppose the next step is for us to spend longer periods of time together—like this weekend—which we're already doing."

"So it's just the house that intimidates you?"

"Uh....yeah."

"I see."

She squirms in her seat. "I guess I wouldn't feel comfortable with you staying at my apartment, either, to tell you the truth."

"Why not? I told you I'm used to it."

"You've worked hard to get where you are. I would feel like you were downgrading—that I was holding you back from enjoying the fruits of your labor."

"What about staying in a different apartment?"

"I would still feel like I was imposing on you and causing you to take a step back from where you should be. I would feel like you were stooping."

I scoff at her across the table. "I would never stoop, Jocelyn. Being with you is not stooping. Being with you anywhere is not stooping in any respect. Please."

"You know what I mean. I would feel like I was holding you back."

"Then be with me at my place. Why do you feel you aren't worthy to enjoy the luxury of my lifestyle? You know you're good enough to be with me in any other context. Take this resort, for example. You don't feel unworthy to be with me here, do you?"

She shifts in her seat again. "I guess not. I just have to keep reminding myself that I'm with you. I'm not here to spend the weekend with the resort."

"You wouldn't be spending the weekend with my house, either—but in any case, I would be happy to spend six months or a year living in a different apartment with you until you get more accustomed to the house. I'm sure you'll get used to it soon enough."

She looks away. "I guess I really ought to see it first before I come to any conclusions."

"You'll see my apartment first."

She frowns. "Which apartment?"

"My apartment at the house. I have an apartment in one end of the house. That's where I live. I don't live in the ballroom or the formal dining room or the pool house, for example."

She blinks at me and then looks away. "Oh. I understand now."

I study her across the table. She really must have thought I did live in the formal dining room, ballroom, and pool house.

There's only one way to deal with this. I have to take her to my house and show her. Then she'll really understand. All this anxiety is just the product of her overactive imagination.

I can only imagine how she thinks a billionaire is supposed to live. She probably thinks my bed is as big as her whole apartment. She wouldn't be the first to jump to conclusions.

I decide to take her mind off it by not mentioning my house again for the rest of the evening. We enjoy a beautiful dinner and then I lead her out onto the terrace overlooking the ocean. It's a perfect night with the resort lights shining out onto the beach.

"Shouldn't we go to our room?" she asks.

"We could. There's no rush to do anything. We're on vacation, remember?"

"Getting back to your question about the future...."

"Did you enjoy your time at the gala?" I ask. "Apart from the time when you were talking to Demetrius, I mean?"

Her head shoots up. "Yes! Of course. Everyone was much nicer than I expected."

"You had already met most of the men at the club. Did you think their wives would be horrible?"

"I don't know what I thought. I guess I didn't expect them to be so....well....ordinary. It was mind-blowing to hear where they had all come from and what they had all been doing before they met their husbands—and what the women still are doing now. It's crazy. I admire them."

"I'm sure they think the same thing about you."

"Oh, they do!" she exclaims. "They told me so. They were all blown away when I told them what I did for work and that I had been the one who investigated you for murder. They thought it was wild and topped any of their stories."

"I don't know about that. Some of them have some pretty wild stories."

"None of them is from another country, though."

I put my arm around her. "I am."

She grins at me. "Yeah. You are. I like that about you."

"I'm sure I didn't have nearly as much of a culture shock as you did. I'm not surprised you reacted negatively to it. I would have hated to come here as a child, especially considering the environment you came from. I'm proud of you for overcoming such an obstacle."

She blushes. "It means a lot to me that you accept that about me—and everything else about me."

"Everything about you is what makes you into such an irresistible package, Jocelyn. I don't know why you've convinced yourself that you're damaged goods. You're anything but. The men who rejected you obviously weren't the right men for you if they couldn't see that."

She sinks into my arms. "You must be right. They must have walked away from me so I would be available when you came along."

"Let's go to our room. We can enjoy the view as much there as we can here."

I lead her down the hall and we enter one of the resort's luxury suites. This one also has its own deck leading out to the beach. We can see just as beautiful a view from here.

Gauzy curtains surround the bed. The room is opulent, luxurious, and all the furnishings are modern and pristine.

She sits down on the bed. "This is nice—much nicer than my apartment."

"You deserve the best." I stand in front of her and cup her cheeks to raise her face so I can look at her. "Remember what I said. It will always be you and me no matter where we are."

"I will remember that."

I let go of her and jump onto the bed to land flat on my back. "This bed is like a trampoline. You better not roll over in the night or I might bounce out onto the floor."

She laughs, turns over, and stretches out next to me. "You might bounce toward the middle and land on top of me."

Now she makes me laugh and blush. "That would be a disaster, wouldn't it?"

She lies next to me where I can put my arm around her. She grins down at me. "I like you. I like spending time with you."

I look up at her and get serious real quick. "I love you, Jocelyn. I want us to stay together and build a future together—as much as you're comfortable with."

She starts to get that panicked look in her eyes again, so I pull her in to kiss her. She melts in my arms and we both sink into kissing each other. We can remember who we are like this. We can remember that it's her and me alone together—alone in the world.

Chapter 28: Jocelyn

I get out of Beau's car and immediately spot Diego standing in front of the New York City courthouse. He keeps checking his phone and pacing up and down.

He comes rushing up to me and Beau the minute we show up. "Thank goodness you're here!" Diego exclaims. "My time slot is coming up and I didn't want to go into the courtroom alone. This is so different from testifying against Emerson."

"You can come with us," I tell him. "We've done this before."

"Thank you." He shakes hands with Beau. "How are you, Detective?"

"I'm fine, Mr. Espinosa," Beau replies. "Let's get in there. We don't have much time."

The three of us go inside and check with the bailiff. He lets us into the courtroom and we take our seats in the gallery. It isn't that full because this is just an indictment hearing to establish if the DA has enough evidence to take Demetrius Runyon to trial.

He sits behind the defense table while DA Jillian McAfee gives her opening remarks.

She outlines the evidence that Junior Osmond had already consulted his high school computer science teacher as well as some of his better qualified contacts from the Article One Innovation Competition.

He had already drawn up and shown them designs and the initial code structure for Spiderware. She also lays out the evidence that he may have had one or some of these conversations where Demetrius Runyon could have overheard.

Beau and I have uncovered eyewitness testimony from classmates in the same school year that Demetrius was on social speaking terms with Junior, had walked home with him on more than one occasion, and that they discussed projects related to their computer science class.

The witnesses also confirm that Demetrius knew about Junior's award and knew that he was working on a new project that he thought was even bigger.

We have confirmed that Demetrius knew Junior's usual route home and was intimately familiar with the surrounding neighborhood. Demetrius could have found a hiding place to ambush Junior when no one else was around.

Their social relationship would have given Demetrius the leverage to lure Junior into the alley where his body was found after the murder.

We have also confirmed with some of Romeano Pinkerton's employees that Demetrius was in fact the person who laundered money through the Corner Pocket Pool Hall under the codename *Spiderware*.

Demetrius has no alibi for the time of the murder. He is also a registered firearms owner of the caliber of weapon the Medical Examiner indicates was used to kill Pinkerton.

Demetrius's lawyer gets up next and goes on a few enormous tangents that make absolutely no sense and don't refute any of the presented evidence against the defendant. I sure as hell hope he doesn't plan to use this as his defense. He'll be screwed if he does.

The attorney for the defense finishes his opening remarks if I can even call them that. He sits down and Jillian calls me to the stand.

The clerk swears me in. Jillian asks me a bunch of questions about my line of inquiry leading to the discovery that Junior was the one who came up with the original concept and code structure for Spiderware.

She specifically asks me how I discovered that Demetrius was one of Pinkerton's money-laundering clients.

I go through the sequence of events from tracking down Pinkerton's ledgers and drawing up a list of his clientele and me spotting the name Spiderware in the ledger.

"So you didn't initially consider Mr. Runyon a suspect?" she asks.

"I had no idea if he even was one of Mr. Pinkerton's clients. I figured anyone might have used that name. Someone could have used the name to implicate Mr. Runyon or someone else from Spiderware could have used the name to cover up illegal activity in their personal life. I had no idea if I should consider Mr. Runyon a suspect or not."

"What led you to make the connection to Junior Osmond?"

"I knew Mr. Runyon was a member of The Billionaires' Club, so I asked some contacts I knew in the club from a previous case to let me attend one of their meetings so I could get more information about him."

"Did you have any notion at the time that someone other than Mr. Runyon may have developed the Spiderware operating system?"

"No. I had no notion at all that it might be the case. It was only much later that I realized that Mr. Runyon had essentially gone from being a penniless high school dropout in the South Bronx to running his own tech company in Manhattan. It didn't make sense that he could have come up with the software overnight—which is what he would have had to do if he really had developed the software on his own. He didn't distinguish himself in computer science at school—not the way Junior did. That was another big tip-off. Their high school computer science teacher barely remembered Mr. Runyon at all, but the teacher couldn't stop talking about Junior almost twenty years after his death. Junior seemed like a much better candidate for being the original developer. The teacher actually got tears in his eyes when he talked about Junior's tragic death right at the point where he might have been able to do something with the software like maybe take it public. That raised my suspicions more than anything—almost as if the killer had been watching him, monitoring his progress, and let Junior work on the program as long as possible before the killer took him out."

"Thank you, Detective." Jillian sits down and the attorney for the defense stands up. I don't recognize the guy. I don't even know his name. He's a nobody, which means he'll be totally unqualified to defend Demetrius against Jillian. She's a tiger in the courtroom.

"At this point, Detective, all your evidence against my client is still entirely circumstantial, isn't it?" the joker asks.

"I guess if you want to call it that, then yes, it is."

"Did you pursue any other lines of inquiry other than carrying out this witch hunt against my client?"

"We pursued lines of inquiry against several of Clemente Barraco's personnel and even against Barraco himself. We had a laundry list of over five hundred suspects at the beginning. We had to eliminate all of them before we pursued any line of inquiry against anyone."

"How did you eliminate them?"

"We started out by finding out which of them had alibis for the night of the murder. We narrowed the list down to fifty who didn't have alibis."

"And did you find any evidence that led you to consider them suspects?"

"None as compelling as this. You might call this all circumstantial evidence, but it does indicate a motive."

"Did any of Clemente Barraco's people have motives to murder the victim? Did you find any motive that Barraco himself had a motive to murder the victim?"

"Actually it was the other way around. They all had motives to keep the victim alive. The victim was an essential money-maker for Barraco's organization. Barraco had no reason to kill the victim or to order any of his people to kill the victim. I guess that's what led us to investigate Mr. Runyon. He was the one who did have a clear motive—a very compelling motive."

"No further questions for this witness at this time." He sits down.

"You may step down, Detective," the judge tells me.

I go sit down. "You did great," Diego murmurs under his breath. "I wish I could be as cool and collected as you."

"Just don't take any of his cross examination too personally. It doesn't mean a thing."

"I wish I could believe that."

Jillian stands up again. "The prosecution calls Diego Espinosa to the stand."

He goes up to the witness box and the clerk swears him in. He acts perfectly composed through the swearing in and while he takes his seat. No one would ever guess he was nervous at all.

He keeps his eyes slightly narrowed, his lips stiff, and he keeps clenching his jaw. Those are the only signs that he's stressed by this circumstance.

Jillian stands up to address her questions to him. "You did business with Mr. Runyon five times since he first joined The Billionaires' Club, didn't you, Mr. Espinosa?"

"Yes, Ma'am, I did."

"Could you outline the nature of these contracts for us, please?"

"I brokered the sale and roll-out of Spiderware software to each of the clients, including the Pentagon, the Chinese National Space Administration, the British House of Parliament, and two civilian corporations that wished to use the software. I used my contacts to facilitate these transactions, whether they were initiated by Spiderware or the client."

"Were you completely satisfied with Mr. Runyon's conduct during these transactions?"

"Yes, Ma'am. I was completely satisfied."

"And you considered Mr. Runyon a good business partner right up until the time when Detective Hitchcock told you that Spiderware's name had come up in this murder investigation. Would I be correct in that conclusion, Mr. Espinosa?"

"Yes, Ma'am. I never had any reason to question Mr. Runyon's integrity or business acumen before that time."

"Did Mr. Runyon do anything, either by action or omission, that might have indicated to you that he was not the original developer of the software? For example, did he ever behave in a way that exempted him from explaining or using the software in a way that would have raised that suspicion?"

"No, Ma'am, I never saw anything like that—but then again, our interactions were always of a business negotiation nature. We spent that time discussing the business aspects of each contract and the logistics of the rollout. I can't remember a time in any of these con-tract negotiations that required Mr. Runyon to use the software or to demonstrate his proficiency at it. That wasn't the nature of the negotiation."

"You were a party to the contract brokering Spiderware software to SigmaTech, were you not?"

"Yes, Ma'am, I was. SigmaTech was one of the civilian companies I mentioned earlier."

"And part of this deal required Spiderware to provide People, Inc. with experts in the Spiderware operating system so People, Inc. could train SigmaTech personnel on how to run the operating system. Isn't that correct?"

"Yes, Ma'am. That's correct."

"These trainers did have to demonstrate their expertise in the software, didn't they? It would have been glaringly obvious to anyone if any of them didn't understand the operating system and had perhaps fraudulently passed himself or herself off as an expert when they weren't one. Isn't that correct?"

"Yes, Ma'am, but I think you can understand that Demetrius was never one of these expert trainers. He was never involved in training SigmaTech people on the operating system, therefore he never was in a position to demonstrate his expertise in it—not in my presence, at least. Neither of the SigmaTech counterparties noticed anything out of the ordinary, either—not that they mentioned to me."

"Thank you, Mr. Espinosa. Nothing further." Jillian sits down.

The joker for the defense stands up. "You mentioned that you considered Mr. Runyon a good businessman and you would have done business with him again had he not gotten singled out for this malicious prosecution. Isn't that your testimony, Mr. Espinosa?"

"Objection!" Jillian interrupts.

"Rephrase the question, Mr. Alcott," the judge orders. That must be the joker's name. Alcott.

"You considered Mr. Runyon a good businessman, didn't you? Would you consider doing business with him again?" Alcott asks. "You claim he never gave you any reason to question his integrity before the prosecution brought these charges."

"Well, one of the clauses of our contracts was that Spiderware warranted that they were the original proprietary copyright holder on the software and that the company did have the legal right to license it for third-party use. So if you want to get technical about it, he did violate that clause—assuming it's proved that he did get the software from someone else."

"No further questions, Your Honor." Alcott returns to the defense table to sit down.

"You're excused, Mr. Espinosa." The judge looks at his watch. "Court is adjourned until two o'clock this afternoon."

Diego stands up and steps down from the witness box. Jillian and her assistant DA talk together and start gathering up their files on this case.

Demetrius and his attorney share a whispered conversation with their heads together. Beau and I stand up and I take a few steps forward to meet up with Diego. I smile at him. I can't wait to tell him how well he did. He dealt with all those questions perfectly.

He meets my eye, and at that moment, I catch a glimpse of movement to one side.

The bailiffs move in to take Demetrius back into custody during the recess. They pull his arms behind his back to cuff him so they can lead him out of the courtroom.

Right then, a different man stands up right behind the defense table. The guy has been sitting in the first row on that side of the gallery. I didn't notice the guy before, but he's one of the only other people in the gallery.

He takes advantage of the commotion in the room to pull a handgun from under his trench coat. He starts to bring it up to aim it at Demetrius.

I don't recognize the assailant. I know a lot of Barraco's men. This isn't one of them.

I don't need to know who he is. He's about to shoot Demetrius right here in the courtroom. I veer sideways and take a flying leap to tackle the guy.

The bailiffs see the shooter at the same time and pull Demetrius out of the way. The bailiffs don't have time to do anything more than that.

I collide with the gunman, wrap my arms around his shoulders to try to stop him from aiming at anything, and we both topple. He falls backward, slams into the bench behind him, and rolls off.

He lands on top of me and the gun goes off somewhere between us. A sickening impact hits me in the chest right at the base of my sternum. A jet of fire blasts straight through me and out through my back.

I hold onto the assailant with all my might, but I can't think straight as darkness takes over my mind and everything goes cold, dark, and silent.

I hear someone calling my name in the distance and then the world disappears.

Chapter 29:
Diego

I pace up and down in front of the swinging doors leading into the emergency surgery department at Mount Sinai Hospital. Beau sits in the waiting area chairs nearby. He watches me pace while he knits his hands together in tense agitation.

Jocelyn has been back there in surgery for hours. No one will come to tell me if she's even going to make it.

How could today end so badly? How could she actually get shot trying to save a lowlife piece of trash like Demetrius Runyon?

The horror of seeing her get shot through the chest and back hovers before my eyes. I can't believe the human body has that much blood in it.

Her quick thinking and sudden attack took down the assailant long enough for the bailiffs to apprehend him and drag him off into custody.

He's in the New York City Jail right now being held without bail for attempted murder of a Police officer. The DA will bump that up to murder if Jocelyn dies—but I don't let myself think that. She can't die. I refuse to accept that.

Beau and I don't talk hour after hour. I ought to sit down next to him. He knows her better than I do. They've been partners for years. I see him getting emotional at the thought of losing her. I should comfort him, but I can't.

Another hour passes before Jocelyn's brother Nicholas comes into the waiting area. He's alone. He doesn't bring his family with him, of course.

He's a heavy-set man in his thirties. He comes in wearing dirty work clothes like he just got the call in the middle of a construction job or something.

I introduce myself to him and I also introduce him to Beau. Nicholas only nods when I tell him that Jocelyn and I have been seeing each other for the last few months while the investigation has been going on.

He sits down with Beau. I keep pacing, but in a little while, the horrible tension becomes too much for me to bear. I sit down next to Beau. He squeezes my shoulder and pats me on the back. He shouldn't be the one comforting me.

I lean forward, rub my hands, and prop my elbows on my knees. I'm just trying to make up my mind how to ease this terrible strain when the doors open. Four male doctors come out still wearing their scrubs.

Nicholas, Beau, and I stand up. "Which one of you is Detective Hitchcock's next of kin?" one of the doctors asks.

"Uh....I am," Nicholas replies. "But these guys can hear your report, too. How is she?"

"She's holding on for the moment. The bullet partially severed her spinal cord, so we won't know how bad the damage will be until she starts to recover. She may be partially or totally paralyzed from the chest down or she may recover her full functioning. We just have to wait and see. The trauma and tissue damage to her chest is severe and she's still in danger, but she's out of surgery and in ICU. You should be able to see her in a few hours."

The three of us collapse into the seats again. All the fight goes out of me when those words ring in my ear. *Partially severed spinal cord*. She'll be partially or totally paralyzed—or she might not be.

This is catastrophic—but what did I expect from her getting shot in the chest? At least she's alive—for now.

I rest my elbows on my knees again. I couldn't pace if I tried. I need to see her—just once. I need to see her once more in case she dies after all.

God only knows what will happen to me if she does. I don't know how I would survive that.

Maybe I wouldn't. Maybe we're so linked now that I would die with her. My body might keep living and going through the motions, but the only part of me that matters will die with her. I can't even care about that.

I just want her to live. She means too much to me. I don't care what condition she's in. I don't care if she's paralyzed. I just want her. I want any part of her I can get even if it means I can't do anything more than talk to her and take care of her.

I'll take care of her for the rest of her life. I don't give a damn what the rest of the world says. I'll never find any woman I love as much as I love her.

I should have told her at the courthouse. I should have told her when she spent the weekend at my house. I should have told her at the resort. I should have told her in a thousand places in a thousand ways.

I should have told her on our very first date. I knew and I didn't say anything because I didn't want to scare her off. I should have told her then and there that she was the one and I wanted to spend the rest of my life with her. Now I might never get a chance to tell her at all.

I should tell Nicholas. That's the bottom line. He's her brother—the only one of her relations that matters.

I stand up and walk around Beau to sit on Nicholas's other side. He glances at me and goes back to staring straight ahead. I'm starting to understand what she said about how he doesn't react to anything. He just accepts everything at face value.

"Listen to me, man," I begin. "I need.....to talk to you....about Jocelyn...."

"I'm sure you probably know her better than I do," he mutters. "She and I haven't exactly been close these last few years since she joined the Force. She became a completely different person after that."

"I....I know." I can't wait any longer. I have to do this now before someone comes out and tells me that she's dead.

I stick my hand in my pocket and pull out the ring box. I've been carrying it around for weeks. I had it with me that night at the resort. I had it with me the whole weekend she spent at my house. Why in the name of God didn't I ask her then?

I can't make that mistake again—not when I'm sitting right next to her brother. I might not get another chance. I crack open the ring box and hold it out for him to see.

"I....I've been holding off.....I don't know why.....I should have asked her weeks ago.....I'm a coward.....but I love her. I love her more than anything. I don't want to lose her....even if I only have a few minutes with her....."

"You should do it," he murmurs. "She needs someone who cares about her that much. Do it."

I shut the box, put it in my pocket, and turn away fighting back tears. I can't fall apart now. She might be fine—except that she won't be. She got shot through the chest and now she's in ICU with a partially severed spinal cord. She isn't fine and she won't be fine.

I'll be fine as long as she survives. I shut my eyes and send up a silent prayer that she just survives long enough to leave the hospital.

I pray she'll make it through all her surgeries and recovery and that she's still alive when this is all over with—alive enough for me to talk to her. I don't ask for anything else. I just want to look into her eyes, talk to her, and know that she's still in the world with me.

I open my eyes and lean forward to prop my elbows on my knees. I don't know what to do with myself.

I'm just making up my mind to go back to pacing when a wheelchair stops in front of me. I look up and find Giovanni Nowaczyk looking into my eyes. Dante, Jackson, Lane, and Kevin are all with him, but Giovanni is the one who commands my attention.

He went through all of this. He almost died on the operating table, went through two painful years of rehab and recovery, and now he's stronger, happier, and more successful than ever.

He grips my shoulder hard enough to bring tears to my eyes. He offers me one small shred of hope that Jocelyn will make it through this. The other guys stare down at me with their eyes brimming over with compassion and concern.

I'm too far out of my mind with worry to think straight, so Kevin steps into the breach. He introduces himself to Nicholas, introduces all the other guys, and introduces Lane and Giovanni to Beau. Kevin introduces them as my friends.

They all shake hands with each other and Beau repeats what the doctor said about Jocelyn's condition. I can't even say a word.

Giovanni stays near me in his wheelchair. Is this a picture of things to come? I don't know half of what he does in his personal life to stay functional. I don't know how he moves around, how he takes care of himself, or how he conducts his private life with Mila.

She's blind, so Giovanni is heavily involved in helping take care of her just as she's heavily involved in taking care of him. They're one of the strongest, most intimate couples I've ever met. Is that what my life will be like with Jocelyn after this?

I would give everything I own and all my wealth to have that with her. I would give everything I own to have any kind of life with her. I would gladly live in the shittiest apartment in New York as long as she was there.

The guys talk about the shooting. Beau fills them in on how it happened and how Jocelyn got shot saving Demetrius Runyon's life when he was on trial for two counts of premeditated murder.

Beau passes his hand across his eyes. "I ain't never even heard of something like that. That's like the stuff of legend in the Force."

I don't tell him that it's just the way she is. She does the job. She does what's right. That's her.

The eight of us are still standing there at loose ends when a nurse comes out of the back. "Which one of you is Diego Espinosa?" she asks.

"Um....I am," I stammer. "Is Jocelyn Hitchcock all right?"

"She's just waking up and she's asking to see you. You can go on in. She's in bed 15J."

She leaves. All the other guys come with me when I go into the back. I don't even care that they're about to see me propose to Jocelyn. I don't care about anything as long as I get the ring onto her finger before she dies on me.

The whole group of us goes into her room. She lies on the bed with a massive bandage around her chest. Her untied gown hangs open so we can see the bandage. She looks weak and frail, but at least she's alive.

She can barely turn her head to see us when we walk in. She smiles at her brother and then at Beau—and then she turns to me.

I sit down on the edge of the bed next to her, pick up her limp hand, and kiss it. I can't stop the tears from springing to my eyes. I don't even see the men standing behind me.

"I love you," I husk. "I should have told you a thousand times. I love you more than anything."

She smiles at me. "It was worth it," she whispers. "If anything happens to me, I want you to know it was worth it. Remember that. Remember it for me."

I nod fighting back tears, but they come anyway. "Marry me." I can't speak above a whisper. "Marry me right now—before anything happens."

She can't move except to smile at me. "I love you. I love you for all time. It will always be just you and me no matter what. Don't forget that, okay?"

I nod again. I'm running out of time, so I take the ring out of my pocket and put it on her finger. She doesn't even look at the ring. She keeps smiling at me. She can't lift her hand to touch my face, but I know she would if she could. Her eyes do it for her.

"I'm tired, Diego," she whispers and her eyes start to drift shut. "I need to go to sleep. I'll see you....."

A loud beep startles me out of my senses. It goes on and on and doesn't stop. Then another alarm goes off on the equipment nearby. I jump to my feet still holding onto her hand.

She doesn't wake up. Her hand feels especially limp in my grasp all of a sudden. "Jocelyn?!" I call. "Jocelyn!!"

She doesn't respond—and then the world caves in when a bunch of nurses and other medical people flood the room. Some of them start pushing the guys outside.

"Jocelyn!!" I hear my voice rising. I can't lose her—not yet. I have to marry her first even if our whole married life only lasts a couple of minutes.

Three medics grab me and tear me away from her. More medical people surround her bed. One of them rips her gown off and starts doing compressions on her right in front of me.

"JOCELYN!!" I roar, but it's too late. The medics push me out of the room. Beau, Nicholas, Jackson, and Dante grab me to stop me from rushing back in there.

They shove me away and practically drag me back to the waiting room. Jackson, Dante, Lane, and Kevin stand in front of me to block me from going near the doors. Beau and Nicholas sit down to wait some more.

I can't wait and I can't pace. I have to get back to her. I need her too badly. I've needed her ever since I first found out she existed. I can't live without her—and now I have to.

Giovanni rolls over to me and clasps his hand around my arm just above the wrist. "Come over here and sit down, brother." He pulls me toward the chairs.

Don't ask me how he does everything so effortlessly. I can't even think straight and he's handling this like a boss.

He pulls me down to make me sit in the chair. Then he plants himself in front of me, locks his hand on my shoulder, and leaves it there. The other four keep standing guard over us. The time drags. Now I really know Jocelyn is in danger.

I can't protect her from this. I want to kill the person who did this to her, but that won't help her, either.

It was worth it. That's what she said. She wants me to remember that. She would gladly sacrifice her life for what she knows is right. If she dies, she'll have died in the line of duty doing what was right.

She protected a man who may well have been innocent—as innocent as I am of Montgomery Sinclair's murder. Demetrius is innocent until proven guilty. He is as deserving of protection as I am.

That's her job. She did her job and it was worth it. Who am I to argue with that?

I just want her. I want her for myself. I want her in my life. Is that asking too much?

How could the world be so cruel as to send her into my life and then snatch her away just when she starts to be so important to me? How am I supposed to accept that?

Chapter 30: Jocelyn

I pry my eyes open and immediately regret it when I feel the crushing weight in the center of my chest. Why do I even have to be alive right now?

I get the answer when I see Diego sitting on the edge of my hospital bed. I feel like absolute shit. I feel like I really wish I was dead, but I can't be when I see all the anguish and excruciating love pouring out of his eyes. He doesn't try to hide it.

I can't even smile at him. My heart cracks with love for him. This pain in the center of my chest—it has nothing to do with the gunshot wound or anything else. It's love—pure love for him.

That love has been fighting to come out all these months. Now nothing can stop it. It overwhelms everything else. I need him and he needs me. I would have to stay alive if only for him—so I can feel this for him.

He raises my hand since I'm too weak to do it for him. He kisses my knuckles—right next to the engagement ring on my finger. I barely see it, but I know it's there. I can't ignore it.

I said I would marry him. I just don't know how I can. Part of me senses myself already slipping away from him. I don't want to, but invisible skeletal hands keep clawing at me and trying to pull me back down into the dark.

Am I dying? I feel like it. I don't feel like I'm part of this world anymore.

Just lying here looking at him—I feel again that it was all worth it. Every day, every challenge, every heartbreak, every defeat—they were all worth it. Life was worth it.

It was all worth it so I could be here to feel this love and see the way he's looking down at me—like I'm the greatest treasure in the world. He looks at me like I'm the most angelic creature ever to set foot on the planet.

I know he thinks that about me. He shows me every day in everything he does and says. He doesn't think he's stooping by being with me. He thinks he's reaching for the stars. He hardly dares to believe his good fortune that he even knows me and gets to hold my hand.

Movement draws my attention to the other side of the room. My brother Nicholas stands on the other side of my bed with Beau. Beau fights back emotion, too. This is hard for him, but the invisible hands won't leave me behind for his sake.

He can always get another partner, but I still wish I could stick around to help him.

My brother is always there. He'll keep being there and going along supporting his family and holding up the world after I'm gone.

Three other people stand across the room—Kevin Drake, Dante Helme, and Jackson Metcalf.

They have to move out of the way when a minister in a black suit and white collar comes in carrying a Bible. I turn back to Diego. He's the only one who matters.

The minister stops next to the bed, offers a blessing on everyone present, and starts reciting the wedding service. This is it. I'm marrying

Diego. This moment right here—this might be all we have. I can live with that.

The minister goes through the whole service and reads out the vows. He asks Diego if he solemnly swears to love, honor, and cherish me, for richer or for poorer, in sickness and in health, for better or for worse, as long as we both shall live.

Diego's eyes overflow with tears and he chokes out, "I do."

Then minister starts asking me the same question. So much love floods me when I look up into Diego's face spasming with emotion. He loves me. I never have to doubt that. If I die right now, I'll die surrounded in more love than I ever imagined possible.

What else is life for except to feel this way about someone and to know just from the look in his eyes that he feels this way about me? I'm everything he's ever wanted. I'm his answer just as he is mine.

The minister asks me if I solemnly swear to love, honor, and cherish Diego, for richer or for poorer, in sickness and in health, for better or for worse, as long as we both shall live.

I can barely speak above a whisper to say, "I do." I've never meant any words more than that. I love him more now than anyone has a right to love anyone. I honor him as the best of men.

I cherish his precious heart. I cherish everything about him, especially how much this means to him. He sits in front of me with tears pouring down his cheeks.

He knows I still have one foot over there in the other world. He knows about the invisible hands. I don't have to tell him. He must sense the hands trying everything in their power to pull me away from him.

The minister asks Diego if he has the ring. He takes a ring box out of his pocket and slips a gold wedding band on my finger to nestle next to the engagement ring he's already given me.

The band has diamonds studded around the circumference. The two rings match each other and make a glittering flash of brilliance on my hand. I would never be able to wear these if I went back out on duty on the street.

I won't go back out. I'll never work in homicide again after this if I even survive at all. The invisible hands don't want me to wear these rings anywhere but my grave.

Diego kisses my hand again right next to the ring. The minister doesn't ask me if I have a ring to give Diego. I couldn't even raise my hand to touch his face, let alone put a ring on his finger.

The minister skips that part and tells us we are now man and wife. The minister gives Diego permission to kiss the bride.

He bends down, gives me the lightest possible kiss on the lips, and then gives me a much longer, more heartfelt kiss on the forehead.

I don't even have the strength to turn my head to see how Beau, Nicholas, and the three billionaires react to this wedding service. It was hardly a wedding, but Diego and I are married now.

Now I can rest. I can let my eyes sink shut and fall into the darkness. Everything will be okay now because I experienced the love of ages—the only love that makes life worth living.

I wake up after what feels like years. My body doesn't ache as much. I just feel impossibly heavy and tired.

I pry my gluey eyes open and see Diego sitting in a chair by my bed. He's alone. He's the only person in the room. He's working on his laptop which rests on the mattress next to me. He goes back and forth between the computer and his phone.

He jumps a foot in the air when I start to open my eyes. He grabs the computer, moves it off the bed to the rolling table nearby, and puts his phone down before he comes back to sit on the edge of my bed.

"Ah! You're awake! Wonderful!" he exclaims and clasps my hand.

I can move around, but barely. I feel drained. Every movement costs all my strength. "What happened?" I rasp. "How long have I been asleep?"

"About a month," he tells me.

I practically scream. "A month! Why?! Why am I still in the hospital?"

"Oh, we got lucky with you," he remarks. "You coded four different times. No one expected you to live. Oh, wait. Beau and Nicholas both want me to call them when you wake up."

He sits next to me while he makes two phone calls. He won't stop smiling at me.

"What the hell happened to me?" I ask when he hangs up. "Why was I.....?"

"You got shot, sweetheart," he chides. "It's a miracle you're alive at all. It's so wonderful that you made it! I was so worried."

He kisses my hand and then my forehead. I try to push myself up, but I can't move my legs. "Am I paralyzed or something? What's wrong with my legs?"

"We don't know. The bullet went straight through the middle of your chest. It did a lot of lung damage, but fortunately, it missed your heart. It severed your spinal cord, but only partially. The doctors say we won't know how much functionality you'll have in your lower body. You just have to go through recovery and find out."

"Great," I grumble and collapse back on the bed with a groan. "Just great."

"This is fantastic!" he gushes. "This is the greatest day! None of us thought you would live—and now the doctors are certain you're going to survive! It's a miracle!" He bursts out in excited laughter. "I have to call Giovanni. He'll be thrilled."

"Giovanni....Nowaczyk?"

"Yes, of course. He's been so supportive. You should talk to him. He went through two years of rehab when he lost the use of his legs and now look at him. Looking at him, talking to him, and watching him—it really gives me hope. I know everything is going to be okay because of him."

I glare at him. "You can't expect me to be happy about becoming paralyzed."

He only smiles at me. "We don't know if you're going to be paralyzed, my darling. You might get everything back. Keep your spirits up. You can't expect me to be upset that you're alive here with me—and now you're my wife. I'm going to be around for a long time to annoy the shit out of you with my sunny attitude."

He laughs again and kisses me on the mouth this time. "Can you please stop being so happy?" I snarl.

He only laughs and calls Giovanni. Diego gets super excited and even happier when he tells Giovanni that I'm awake. Diego doesn't tell Giovanni that I woke up on the wrong side of the bed.

I try again and again to move my legs, but nothing happens. I can't move anything from the gunshot wound down. This is a nightmare, but Diego couldn't be happier.

He makes a bunch of other phone calls and even gets emotional during some of them because this is such a great day. I guess I can't resent him for being happy that I made it.

Things settle down pretty soon. The medical team comes in, takes my vitals, and does an assessment on my lower body. I still have full sensation everywhere. I just can't move.

One of the doctors pulls the blankets off my feet. "Wiggle your toes," he tells me.

I wiggle my toes. I can still do that much.

Diego goes into hysterics of even more happiness when he sees that. He claps his hands and bursts out in laughter. "This is fantastic! Don't you see what this means? You still have at least partial functioning in your legs! You could get it all back!"

"Let's continue to be cautiously optimistic," the doctor tells him. "Ms. Hitchcock still has to go through a long recovery before we know how much movement she'll have."

Diego won't stop beaming at everyone, especially me. The medical team leaves and we wait another five or six hours. Nothing happens. He goes back to working on his laptop.

He fields a bunch of phone calls and even does a few video meetings from the hospital room to keep running his business. I fall asleep more than once, but I always wake up. He's always there when I open my eyes. He's always happy to see me.

He has to raise and lower my bed so I can eat. I have a colostomy bag and a catheter so I don't have to go to the bathroom.

The doctors come back the following day to tell me I'll have to recover most of my strength before they'll take either of them out and return me to normal.

I moan and groan about it a lot, but Diego sails right through it all as delighted as ever. "I just don't care, sweetheart. I really, honestly just don't care as long as you're here. You don't know how many times I prayed for you to survive. I never cared what condition you were in as long as you stayed here with me where I could look into your eyes and talk to you. I never asked anything else and I never will. Whatever you want from me, whatever you need—I'm right here. You and your precious heart are all I need."

I hesitate. "Diego?"

"Yes, my love?" he breathes.

"The doctor....."

"Yes? What about him?"

"He said...he called me, '*Ms.* Hitchcock'."

Diego understands instantly, sits down next to me, takes my hand, presses it, and lowers his voice to murmur in a low, confidential undertone. Of course he understands.

"You're retired from the Force, my love. You're on a disability pension for the rest of your life. I'm sorry, but you'll never return to active duty even if you do make a full recovery."

I look away. Of course it would come to that, but it still stabs me in the guts. I won't go back to active duty. My life will never be the same.

He stays there holding my hand for a long time. I want to lash out at someone. I want to get angry and hurt someone for this, but I can't take it out on him even though I want to.

Being a cop gave me a life. It gave me confidence. It gave me a way to bridge the gap between me and other people when I didn't have that. It gave me a sense of myself as a professional on par with others.

I never would have been able to talk to Diego and build a relationship with him without that. I wouldn't have had the confidence to do anything with him or even have a conversation with him if I had still been working as a diner waitress.

I spend the next four weeks in the hospital. Beau visits a lot. He has a new partner and comes to rant to me about what a bumbling idiot the guy is.

"Give the kid a break," I tell him. "I'm sure we were all clumsy and awkward when we first got out of the Academy."

I also get a few visits from my brother. We don't have a lot to say to each other. We talk about his family. That's the only thing we have to talk about anymore.

Diego gets a lot of visits from his friends in The Billionaires' Club. They all super friendly and supportive to him and to me. I'm getting to know them all so much better now.

Giovanni Nowaczyk comes the most often. Diego is right. Seeing how strong and confident Giovanni is sure is inspiring to me to keep going.

His wife Mila just gave birth to their first child. Giovanni is thrilled to be a father. Life won't be that bad even if I am paralyzed.

Then comes the inevitable day when one of the hospital physical therapists comes to see me. Diego helps me sit up and pull my legs to the edge of the bed.

The therapist puts a walker in front of me. Diego stands next to me and takes my hand so I can lean my weight on him.

"Great. I'm using a walker now," I grumble. "I'm an old lady."

He laughs at me. I heave myself off the bed and push my weight onto my legs while I hold onto the walker. My arms tremble. I'm a lot weaker than I realized.

"Just remember it took Giovanni two years to get strong enough to do what he does with his arms," Diego tells me.

"You won't have to hold yourself up like this if you get back the use of your legs," the therapist adds. "Concentrate on that."

Holding myself up like this exhausts me, but I can still take a few steps. It's hard, but at least I can put my weight on my legs and move them. I guess life could be a lot worse.

The visits from friends and family tail off after a while. People don't come as often, now that they see I'm going to survive. Life is starting to return to normal even if it wasn't what it used to be.

Diego leaves my hospital room more often to tend to his business, but he always comes back.

"Wouldn't you rather stay at home?" I ask. "It can't be very comfortable for you here."

He smiles at me. "It isn't. That's why the doctors are releasing you at the end of the week."

My head shoots up. "They are?"

He beams down at me. "I'm taking you home......wife." He laughs at that word, kisses me on the head, and hugs me against him. "Congratulations. You'll be able to continue your recovery from home."

The doctors perform the surgery to reverse my colostomy and remove the catheter on Wednesday. I have my work cut out for me just getting to the bathroom and back to bed each time. That's all the exercise I can handle at this point.

Being in a coma for a month, going through multiple life-threatening surgeries, and crashing on the operating table four times has left me weak—much weaker than I was when I went into this.

I have to get a lot stronger to be able to move myself onto and off the bed. I have to build up my arm strength to be able to push myself up on my walker and hold myself there while I move my legs.

It's a good thing I have such a great role model. Giovanni comes by and shows me how he does everything by sliding himself across a board from one seat to another or pivoting himself with his arms.

He blows my mind by showing me how he climbs ladders with his arms and climbs pegboards and vertical pipes and all kinds of other superhuman stuff. I don't know if I'll ever get as good as that.

I really am much better off than he is. I can use the walker to get out of a wheelchair in the hospital parking garage. I can stand up to pivot into the limo when the time comes for Diego to take me home.

We hold hands on the way. I find myself smiling at him. "I love you," I murmur to him.

"Having you here is a privilege and a blessing. Never forget that. Going through this recovery may be frustrating for you at times, but just remember that. Every day with you is a priceless gift."

I have to remind myself of that a lot nowadays. I especially have to remind myself when I try to do things and find that I can't.

It's easier to remember that life is good when Diego wheels my chair into his apartment at his estate. It's enormous, luxurious, and immaculate. The living room opens onto a magnificent garden adjacent to the grounds of the rest of the estate.

He's added a bunch of features to make the apartment more wheelchair accessible so I can get around more easily. I won't be wheelchair-bound forever. I just need to get stronger before I stop using the walker.

I get a home visit from the physical therapist once a week. I have to do all my work and exercises on my own the rest of the time.

Just going through some small version of a daily routine is a major workout on its own. Walking across the apartment takes all my strength, but at least I can do it now.

Diego gets back into a normal routine, too. He starts going back to work every morning. That leaves me in the apartment alone to do my exercises.

I have the rest of the day to do what I want. I concentrate on being able to do household tasks like clean the apartment and cook meals for us in the apartment kitchen.

The mansion has a giant commercial kitchen designed to be run by a culinary team and cater to a household of hundreds of people.

Diego uses the mansion and facilities for company events. He doesn't keep a permanent culinary staff on the premises. That would be overkill for just the two of us.

I finally get to the point after six months where I can walk. I have to hitch my body from side to side and swing my legs forward before I can put my weight on each of them. The rest of my life returns to normal. I just walk differently from other people.

"It isn't the most graceful, attractive way to move around, is it?" I ask Diego. "I look like I'm having an epileptic seizure."

He laughs. "I won't lie. It does kind of look like that."

Winter turns to spring. Diego kisses me at the kitchen counter before he leaves for the morning. I do a few chores in the house and then go out onto the terrace to enjoy the warmer weather.

I take my laptop with me to check my email. I freeze when I get an email saying the Police Department is conducting its annual Medal Day to recognize outstanding bravery and dedication. The department wants to recognize me.

I sit rooted to my seat and stare at the screen as the ultimate reality sinks in. I'm not a Police officer anymore. I've been so focused on my recovery that I didn't think about that until now.

I'm just a civilian. I'm not even that. I'm a housewife exactly the way my first boyfriend wanted me to be.

I'm here when Diego comes home. I clean the house and make the meals. I don't have a career. I don't even have a job. I barely have a reason to get up in the morning.

I click away from the email about the awards ceremony, but it's still right there in front of my eyes. I can't stop facing the final insult staring me right in the face.

I've attended these Medal Days every year since I graduated from the Academy. I've sat in the audience and watched my fellow officers get recognized, awarded, and decorated. I've gotten recognized, awarded, and decorated before myself.

I'll attend this ceremony, but not as a Police officer. I won't wear the uniform. I won't sit with the other officers. I'll have to sit with the families, friends, and other civilian employees of the department.

What is my life coming to? I found my calling—and I lost it. Now what am I supposed to do?

I make the worst mistake of my life by navigating to a job search page. The listings include positions for health care administrators, safety and compliance officers for factories and production plants, events coordinators, sound technicians, teachers, nurses, and accountants.

I click away from that and shut my computer. I can't become one of them. I can't become just another person going to a job somewhere. I could never do that.

Every particle of my being tells me to go back out into the field to keep doing Police work. Nothing else makes sense—but I can't. I can't even walk properly.

I need something, though. I can't be a housewife. I can't stand seeing myself as that. It's a violation of everything I am and everything I hold sacred. Life isn't worth living if I'm only that.

I'm still sitting here thinking about it when Diego comes home. He frowns at me. "What are you doing out here? Did something go wrong with your legs?"

"No, nothing went wrong with my legs."

He furrows his brow at me. "Something's wrong, isn't it?"

I tell him about the award. "I never wanted to do any other job. Now what am I supposed to do?"

He sits down across from me on the terrace, opens his mouth to answer, and changes his mind. "No, that would never work."

"I looked up a bunch of job listings earlier. They were all for normal civilian jobs like medical professionals and admin positions. I don't want to do anything like that. The fact that I'm even in a position of thinking about applying for them feels like a slap in the face."

He gazes off into the trees surrounding the estate. "I can understand that. The physical challenge was a big part of what made Police work appealing to you and that's exactly the part of the job you can't do anymore. What about becoming something like a private detective or something like that?"

"Do you mean following cheating husbands around and catching them on camera? No, thank you."

He snorts with laughter. "Okay. Maybe that was a bad idea."

"I was working on homicides, Diego. I was tracking down murderers and coordinating informants inside the mob. I was actually doing some good in the world."

"I know, my love." He glances around. "Let's order dinner in tonight. You have too much on your mind to cook."

He pulls out his phone. I don't look at him while he navigates around to find a restaurant to order from.

I don't tell him I don't want to make dinner ever again. I don't want to be a housewife. That's the last thing in the world I want to be.

It isn't that I don't love living with him and building our life together. I do love that. I just need something more. I need to feel like I'm part of something.

My heart twists for the comrades and community of the Police Department. That was something special. I'll probably never find anything like that again.

I don't want to find anything like that. I want that. I want the department. I want my partners and colleagues and friends. I want to share that danger and all the trouble that came with it. That's why I joined the Force in the first place. I don't want anything else.

I really don't want to wake up tomorrow morning and face another boring day by myself in this apartment. I can't face that.

Diego places the order and calls out to the security guards at the estate's entrance gate to let them know the delivery will be coming in. He goes inside and does a few other things before he comes back with our food.

He beams at me while he spreads it out on the terrace picnic table in front of me. Sometimes I irrationally resent him for being so happy about our lives together.

The times when I'm struggling, frustrated, hopeless, and upset are the times that make him the happiest. He couldn't be happier than just to be there for me and go through it with me. He doesn't want anything else.

He's just sitting down and picking up his chopsticks when he gets another phone call. His expression changes in a heartbeat when he hears the voice on the other end.

"Oh, okay, I see. Well, send them in." He hangs up, puts his phone away, and gets to his feet. "Beau and Sergeant Mayweather are here to see you, my love."

I freeze with my food halfway to my mouth. "Um....what?"

"That was the gatehouse. The two of them are here to see you. Stay here. I'll go get them."

He hustles away. I leave the food where it is, go inside, and stand in the living room waiting for Diego to bring Beau and the sergeant to the apartment. Beau comes to see me all the time. This will be the first time I've seen Sergeant Mayweather since I got shot.

Diego escorts them into our apartment. Beau hugs me and tells me I'm looking so much better, now that I'm walking around.

I shake hands with Sergeant Mayweather. "It's great to see you back on your feet," he tells me. "We really thought we were going to lose you there for a while."

"What's the situation, Sarge?" I ask. "Why did you want to see me?"

"Sit down, Jocelyn," he tells me and he and Beau sit down on the couch.

No one mentions that Sergeant Mayweather is telling me to sit down in my own house. Diego sits down next to me and takes my hand.

"The department would like you to come back to work," Sergeant Mayweather tells me. "You wouldn't be returning to active duty. We would like you to take the role of disabilities coordinator. You would be responsible for distributing benefits, managing caseloads, and assigning services to officers injured in the line of duty and their families—people like you. You would be responsible for ensuring that the injured officers and their families understand the services available to them and that everyone is taking advantage of everything they can take advantage of. You would be responsible for managing the medical care, rehabilitation, and occupational therapy of all our current cases and helping to determine if and when an injured officer can return to work based on their condition and how well they're rehabilitating."

I blink at him in shock. Is this really happening?

He spreads his hands in front of me. "It's a desk job. I know you probably don't want to do that, but we could really use you. We've always had civilians in that post before. This would be the first time the disabilities coordinator actually was a retired, disabled former Police officer. You could bring a degree of compassion and personal experience to the job instead of turning it into just another admin post. The officers on our caseload really need someone like that. They need to see that the person they're dealing with is one of their own who understands what they're going through." He looks away for a second. "It would really be helpful for those officers who, like you, get so injured that they can't return to work. They need someone managing their cases who understands."

Now I'm the one who looks away. I don't want to do a desk job, but that's all I'm qualified for now.

This is it. This is the position I'm supposed to do. I'll be a part of the Police Department again. I'll be working with my fellow officers. They still need me.

It isn't the same as investigating homicides and busting mobsters and murderers, but in a way, it makes even more sense because these officers need me more. The city doesn't need another homicide detective. The department already has enough of those.

The city does need this. These injured and disabled officers and their families need me more than anyone has ever needed me. This is even more important than homicide.

Diego squeezes my hand just then. This is it. It's the answer I've been looking for and it just landed right here in my lap. I didn't even have to go looking for it.

I turn around and face Sergeant Mayweather. "Yeah. I'll do it. I would like that."

"Wonderful." He pulls out his phone. "I'm going to put you in touch with Chief Rodecker and the personnel department. They've been looking for someone for four months, so they'll be thrilled with your qualifications. They'll send you all the paperwork for you to fill out. You'll go through the interview process and everything, but I'm sure you'll sail through easily. We have no other candidates, so you're sure to get the job."

We all stand up and I shake hands with him again. "Thank you for coming by, Sarge. I really appreciate it."

"We're the ones who will appreciate it. I guess I'll see you at the station again pretty soon."

"Yeah!" I find myself laughing in relief. "That would be great."

I hug Beau again and Diego and I head back out to the terrace to eat our food. I feel better than I have since before I got shot.

I'm going back to the Police station. I'm going to work for the department again. I'm going to be involved with my fellow officers and be there to help them when they need me.

Diego only smiles at me across the table. He doesn't have to say a word and neither do I because we both know what this means. I'm back. I can keep being the cop I was before. I can still make a difference where it matters.

That's what my brother and sister officers need and that's what I'm going to do.

Epilogue: Diego

I get out of the limo and wait while Jocelyn slides herself across the seat to join me. She has to take hold of either side of the door frame and use her arms to pull herself to her feet before she straightens up.

She sees me watching her and blushes. "Stop that."

"What?" I ask. "I can gaze in mesmerized admiration of my wife, can't I?"

She giggles. "Don't think I didn't notice the way you were watching me. You can't fool me."

"I have no idea what you're talking about." I hold out my arm and she takes it.

We head into the hotel, but we have to do it slowly. She still walks with a slow, side to side, lurching gait that doesn't look right in her long, sleek fire-engine red gown.

I barely notice the way she walks. It all seems so normal now.

The rest of her looks as stunning as ever. Her eyes shine more brightly since she started working for the Police Department as the new disability coordinator. It makes her even happier than she was when she was a detective.

Lane and Samantha enter the lobby behind us and catch up with us before we get to the ballroom entrance. "Jocelyn—you look fantastic!"

Samantha hugs her and they kiss on the cheeks. Lane and I shake hands.

"You look exhausted," Jocelyn tells Samantha.

Samantha laughs. "This is with a ton of makeup making me look better than I do."

"How's the new rug rat?" I ask.

"He hasn't learned yet that his mother is already married to someone else," Lane replies and we all laugh.

Lane and Samantha stay with us the rest of the way to the entrance and the four of us enter together. We all get lost in the crowd the minute we walk in. Our friends come over to talk to us, greet us, catch up on each other's lives, and the club members talk about business.

The wives talk about business, too. Jocelyn is one of the very few who isn't in business for herself, but she talks as animatedly as the others.

She talks about her work and they all listen in fascination. She listens in fascination when they talk about their work. No one cares that she works for the city. She's family. We all are.

She kisses me on the cheek and goes off toward the buffet with some of the women and a few men. They get into more conversation over there.

No one in the club notices or cares about the way she walks. They slow down to keep pace with her so they can continue their conversation. The love in the room overshadows everything else.

I find myself watching her from afar. She sure has come a long way from the days when she considered all of us cutthroats and manipulators. She even talks to the other gala attendees about contributing to the Police Disability Fund.

She moves as effortlessly here as she did before she got shot. Her job gives her the same sense of ease and professional confidence that she had when I met her. She's a superhero—as much or more than she ever was.

She's still saving the world, especially mine. I'm the lucky devil that gets to take her home after this. I'm the one who gets to make her understand how much we all love and admire the beautiful guardian angel that she is.

<u>End of Book 9.</u>

.

Keep Reading

The Billionaires' Club Series: Book 10: Private Investigation

The Billionaires' Club is under threat—again. Investigative journalist Nicole Bates is on the case and digging up all the gory details of the club's recent troubles. She paints the club as full of dangerous predators who don't care about anything more than screwing everyone over to make money.

The club's PR officer steps in to stop the situation from spiraling out of control. Rory Kahn cracks down on Nicole, but she's about to find out that the club isn't what she thought it was—and neither are any of the people in it. With powerful forces pulling the puppet strings behind the scenes, Nicole and Rory get caught in a whirlwind of political intrigue that could destroy everything they've worked to build.

When circumstances throw Rory andNicole together, they're both going to discover hidden truths about themselves and each other that will leave their worlds in ruins. Can The Billionaires'Club survive this upheaval—and is there any way it can bounce back and become something even greater?

You can find it at your favorite book retailer.

Get All of AE Moran's Free Books

S ign Up Once—Get all A.E. Moran's free books including brand new releases

Holden Seager is hot, magnetic, and filthy, stinking, obscenely rich. He commands a room the minute he walks in the door. So what happens when meets another shark as powerful, as charismatic, and as successful as he is—not to mention ten years younger? When these two meet across the negotiating table, one of them will walk away the undisputed winner. The other will walk away with nothing.

Or so it seems.

Unless they're best friends.

When the business deal of a lifetime falls flat on its face and neither of these titans knows how to bring it back to life, this might be the opportunity Dayna Turner has been waiting for.

There's just one problem. She works as an assistant to one of these powerful men....and she's in love with the other. It's a recipe for disaster and heartbreak—unless Dayna can pull off an even bigger coup that will leave them all richer, happier, and more closely connected than ever. The alternative is the destruction of everything all three of them have worked so hard to build.

Sign up at www.authoraemoran.com to read it for free.

About AE Moran

A.E Moran is the contemporary romance pen name for Theo Mann.

I write 70 books per year—and yes, before you ask, all these books are my original creative work. Nothing written under my name is AI-generated or ghostwritten because I write better than AI and any ghostwriter out there.

People don't read fiction for entertainment or to escape from reality. People read fiction to see their humanity reflected in another person's character and story.

This is my promise to you. When you read my books, you'll see your own humanity reflected in the characters and stories. I take this commitment to my readers very seriously. My books are an intimate form of communication between us. I would never disrespect my readers by turning that over to a machine or another writer. This is my bond between me and you as my reader.

I write 20,000 words per day as my daily work output. If anyone with a public platform would like to challenge me to prove this in a controlled environment, feel free to contact me on this website's contact page.

I worked as a professional ghostwriter for fifteen years. Now I'm going for the Guinness World Record by writing 700 books over the next ten years and 1400 books over the next twenty years, all originally written by me. See my website for the full book list.

I'm also the author of *Proof for the Existence of God* and the *Crimes Against Fiction* blog. You can find all my nonfiction work at www.crimes-against-fiction.com.

If you have a story idea, or if you would like me to explore a series in more depth, or if you'd like me to explore a character by writing a spinoff series about that character or world, leave me a message on my website's contact page. I answer all reader emails, so ask me anything, tell me what you liked and didn't like, and let me know where you'd like your favorite series to go. I would love to hear your ideas and find out what you'd like to read next.

You can find out more at www.theomann.com or at www.authoraemoran.com.

Also by AE Moran (so far)

www.ingramcontent.com/pod-product-compliance
Lightning Source LLC
Chambersburg PA
CBHW052031020726
47501CB00004B/1357